THE LOST BOOK OF ENOCH, JUDGEMENT OF THE WATCHERS

Written by

Melissa Sheridan

The Lost Book of Enoch:
Judgement of the Watchers

Edited by Tom Jolliffe

Cover Design by Adrian Traurig

Author Photograph by Krista Nix

Printed on acid-free paper

Library of Congress Control Number:

ISBN: 978-1-958450-13-0 (PB)
ISBN: 978-1-958450-14-7 (HB)

First Printing: December 2024

Dedication

This script is dedicated to the hubris in all of us—may we continually strip away the prideful elements that do not serve us or others, and instead find the humility to surrender to a higher purpose.

FADE IN:

EXT. BLACK SCREEN

FLASHBACK

A DYING MOTHER cries out in pain. Sound of a newborn crying.

INT. CAVE - NIGHT

SUPER: BEFORE THE GREAT FLOOD

Dying Mother is handed her newborn baby girl, NA'ELTAMA'UK. She soothes the baby's cry with her last breath and names her.

All dialogue in Hebrew.

DYING MOTHER
Na'eltama'uk.

SISTER
That is a beautiful name.

SISTER anoints baby's head with oil.

SISTER (CONT'D)
She is so beautiful.

DYING MOTHER
Promise me. You'll take care of her, please.

Mother dies.

SISTER
No! God, please, no!

SISTER weeps for her dead sister. Baby is taken from Mother's hands by an angelic man, ARMAROS.

In the distance we see YOUNG AVIV (10) and his father AZAZEL, resting his hands on the young boys shoulders.

The two move forward to carry the dead Mother away while her Sister cries out in agony.

Armaros places crying baby in a wooden bed.

MATCH CUT TO:

INT. MUHAMMAD'S HOME - DAY

SUPER: KHIRBET QUMRAN, 1947

FLASH FORWARD

Mother picks up her FUSSY BABY while finishing dinner. She looks out the window with worry.

Emphasis on leather strap necklace with stone that will be of significance later.

EXT. MUHAMMAD'S HOME - DAY

Mom bursts open door and yells for her son who has wandered off too far.

MOM
Muhammad!

She walks back into the home with Fussy Baby on her hip.

MOM (CONT'D)
(Quraish Arabic)
Always running off. What am I going to do with him?

CUT TO:

EXT. CAVE - DAY

A young boy's feet run up the side of a mountain (MUHAMMAD THE WOLF). The feet of a goat run through boulders. Muhammad scales side of mountain to catch his goat.

All dialogue in Quraish Arabic.

MUHAMMAD
Come back here you silly goat!

The goat's cry echoes through the mountains.

MUHAMMAD (CONT'D)
Remember I'm the one who feeds you!

Goat looks at him with almost taunting spirit then runs off.

MUHAMMAD (CONT'D)
(to himself)
You should listen to me or dad will make you for dinner!

Muhammad continues to scale tall mountain. He hears his goat.

He travels toward the sound and stumbles across an opening in the mountain.

Muhammad picks up a small rock and tosses it into a cave to scare his goat out.

MUHAMMAD (CONT'D)
I know you're in there!

Muhammad pauses and sighs.

He throws second rock and hears the sound of a clay jar breaking.

Curiosity takes over, and he slowly moves toward entrance of the cave.

EXT/INT. CAVE - DAY

Muhammad enters the cave, uncovering ancient artifacts, including the jar he broke.

His face lights up as he glances into a jar and sees something wrapped in linen.

MUHAMMAD
Woah.

He continues to carefully rummage through found materials. He unrolls an old scroll with ancient writing on it.

He blows off dust and continues to look at it closely.

Goat calls out behind him. Muhammad is startled.

MUHAMMAD (CONT'D)
Ahhhhhh! There you are.

He ties a rope around the neck of goat to keep him close.

Muhammad glances back at the items, contemplating taking something home with him.

He grabs one scroll.

EXT. MOUNTAINS OF KHIRBET QUMRAN - DAY

Muhammed runs hurriedly down the mountain, pulling his stubborn goat on a rope with one hand and the scroll in the other.

CU on scroll over beginning credits.

There are signs of war. Smoke plumes in the distance.

MOVIE TITLE: THE LOST BOOK OF ENOCH, JUDGEMENT OF THE WATCHERS

Credits continue over Muhammad's journey back home with emphasis on scroll.

CUT TO:

INT. MUHAMMAD'S HOUSE - DINING ROOM - NIGHT

Muhammad, his mom and father finish their dinner around small dining room table. His sister lays in a crib, content. Muhammad tries to eat quickly, avoiding eye contact.

All dialogue in Quraish Arabic.

MOM
Are you going to show your dad that thing you brought home?

Muhammad chokes on his water.

MOM (CONT'D)
What, I'm your mother. I see everything.

MUHAMMAD
I was just...

MOM
You were just going to get it and show it to your father.

Mom smiles. Muhammad sighs and gets up from chair to retrieve scroll.

--

Dad carefully unrolls the scroll on the dining room table as he takes a bite of his dinner.

MUHAMMAD
(Quraish Arabic)
There's more up there father.

Dad examines the scroll. His face is filled with wonder and hope.

DISSOLVE TO:

EXT. MARKETPLACE - DAY

Dad and Muhammad carry multiple scrolls in a goat skinned bag as they travel through a busy marketplace.

We hear sounds of customers bargaining over vegetables. FISH VENDOR is shouting his afternoon sale.

All dialogue in Quraish Arabic.

FISH VENDOR
Fresh fish! Fresh fish!

The merchants watch the two carry their precious cargo as they travel through market, past FRUIT VENDOR

FRUIT VENDOR
Fresh fruits, 3 pounds a bundle!
Fresh fruits!

Muhammad pauses, distracted by a delicious fruit but dad quickly pulls him away.

INT. MARKETPLACE HUT - DAY

TRADER takes a look at the scroll with his magnifying glass.

All dialogue in Quraish Arabic.

DAD
Well?

TRADER
Maybe repurpose the leather.

DAD
Surely there's something here.

Trader rolls up the scroll and hands it back.

TRADER
Take them to the general store. See Kando. He will tell you what to do with them.

CUT TO:

INT. GENERAL STORE OF SYRIAN ORTHODOX MERCHANT - DAY

KANDO looks at the scrolls with great scrutiny.

All dialogue in Quraish Arabic.

KANDO
Hebrew.
(pause)
This could be very old indeed.

Dad smiles.

KANDO (CONT'D)
Are you willing to sell?

Boy smiles.

EXT. MARKETPLACE - DAY

MONTAGE

Scrolls travel with Kando through the marketplace. They are handed off to a MAN ONE who walks with them for some distance.

Man One hands them off to MAN TWO and he walks with them for a distance. He hands them off to another MAN THREE.

MONTAGE ENDS

EXT. GATEWAY TO MILITARY ZONE B - DAY

Dusk. Two men separated by a barbed wire fence.

An ARMENIAN MAN holds up a sample fragment of leather. SUKENIK (Jewish scholar) pulls out his glasses and takes a look.

SUKENIK
Shkran Iak.

INT. BUS - DAY

Sukenik sits on a bus full of ARABS, carrying Hebrew scrolls under his arm, wrapped in ordinary parcel.

DISSOLVE TO:

EXT. MUHAMMAD'S HOME - NIGHT

Dad and Muhammad walk home with their earnings.

All dialogue continues in Quraish Arabic.

MUHAMMAD
Maybe we buy a cow, or some more chickens.
(pause)
Just no more goats.

Dad chuckles.

CUT TO:

INT. SUKENIK'S HOME NIGHT

SUKENIK unrolls a fragile scroll with trembling fingers.

As he pours over text, his radio announces that the United Nations General Assembly has voted in favor of establishment of a Jewish state.

Spontaneous celebrations break out in streets.

EXT. MUHAMMAD'S HOME - NIGHT

Muhammad's family celebrate.

INT. SUKENIK'S HOME - NIGHT

Sukenik continues to look visibly agog at the scrolls. He magnifies text.

SUKENIK
The Book of Enoch.

MATCH CUT TO:

FLASH FORWARD ENDS

INT. ENOCH'S HUT - NIGHT

SUPER: BEFORE THE GREAT FLOOD

ENOCH writes the same text on scrolls of old in Hebrew. The text is first heard in its language of origin but switches over to English for duration of story.

ENOCH (V.O.)
(in Hebrew)
Ben Elohim...
(MORE)

ENOCH (V.O.) (CONT'D)
Beings created by God to be earthly shepherds of the first primitive humans.
(in English)
Everything visible on earth was overseen by the sons of God... The Watchers.

FADE TO:

EXT. SUMMIT OF MOUNT HERMON - DAY

MONTAGE

Blades of wheat blow in fields surrounding Mount Hermon.

TIME LAPSE OF MANY DAYS AND NIGHTS PASS

ENOCH (V.O.)
For years God entrusted them to watch... They watched over mankind willingly and not grudgingly.

Bright lights zoom over land/people.

ENOCH (V.O.)
Not for what they would gain, but eager to serve their God.

TIME LAPSE ENDS

EXT. SUMMIT OF MOUNT HERMON - NIGHT

DIVINE BEINGS walk the earth. An ANGEL OF LIGHT tends to a beautiful garden with dogwood trees.

He applies a layer of suppressed weeds and organic mulch around roots to help tree retain moisture.

ANGEL OF LIGHT TWO watches a field of sheep as ADAM, the first shepherd, rests his head on a nearby rock.

ENOCH (V.O.)
But some of the watchers grew frustrated with God's plan. In their pride and anger, they rebelled against their creator and each other.

Bright lights fall from the sky.

Large feet crush the wheat of the field.

ENOCH (V.O.)
God prepared the bloodline for a messiah... The fallen prepared a plan to stop it.

The fall of man/woman in the garden. A Serpent watches from a tree.

CAIN kills his brother ABEL in a field with a rock.

Presence of DARK FIGURES and the Serpent in the background.

MONTAGE ENDS

FADE TO:

EXT. ANCIENT MEETING SPACE MT. HERMON - NIGHT

ANGELIC BEINGS are gathered around a table draped with black silk.

Some faces are covered in white silk, most in black. FALLEN LEADER, SEMJAZA address the group.

SEMJAZA
He has betrayed us and made plans to bring forth a messiah to the world.

ANGEL IN BLACK SILK leans forward.

ANGEL IN BLACK SILK
Replace us?

Mumbling around the table.

ANGEL IN BLACK SILK (CONT'D)
Have we not given everything to protect mankind? Where is our reward in all this?
(pause)
Do we not deserve to love? To share in our knowledge? Why give us the desire for a woman? Now we need his permission to lay with her? Mankind has everything he could want and need.

A few silk coverings in the group fade from white to black.

SEMJAZA
Who is man but withering grass, a flower that fades...
(MORE)

SEMJAZA (CONT'D)
We are the great ones! And we shall reign over man, victorious!

Another few silk coverings in the group fade from white to black. Mumbling around the table continues.

SEMJAZA (CONT'D)
Can you not see God's presence has abandoned us? But together we will crush man under our feet.

ALL DARK ANGELS
Ay!

SEMJAZA
We must prevent this promised one.

DARK ANGEL leans forward to address the group.

DARK ANGEL
And how do you propose we do that?

SEMJAZA
We will have the daughters of Adam and infiltrate the bloodline. We continue to teach great knowledge that will cause them to rebel against their creator. There will be no promised one.

Semjaza bangs his hands down on table.

SEMJAZA (CONT'D)
Who's with me?!

Some hesitate to answer.

ALL DARK ANGELS
Ay!

SEMJAZA
Some of you say you are, but are not. If you hesitate in your commitment, I ask that you leave.

Semjaza looks around at those who are still in white silk coverings.

SEMJAZA (CONT'D)
I fear you will not indeed agree to continue to do this deed, and I alone shall have to pay the penalty of a great sin... Let us all swear an oath.

Semjaza leans over table.

SEMJAZA (CONT'D)
But to do it!

ANGEL IN WHITE SILK covering stands.

ANGEL IN WHITE SILK
I will not! This plan is blasphemy!

SEMJAZA
You can leave if you choose... And if any one else feels the same, you may go.

Angel in White Silk leaves with others in white silk.

SEMJAZA (CONT'D)
Anyone else?

Looks around.

SEMJAZA (CONT'D)
Good.

CUT TO:

EXT. ANCIENT MEETING SPACE ALTER - NIGHT

Dark angels interlock arms. They chant their commitment.

ALL DARK ANGELS
(Gregorian Chant 440 Hz.)
We swear. All together. And bind ourselves by mutual imprecations upon it.

Semjaza cuts his left palm with a small sharp rock. The rest follow suit.

They all place their left hands on a stone in the middle of a circle. The blood drips down from the stone.

SEMJAZA
With our blood we bind this agreement! And nothing shall break it!

ALL DARK ANGELS
(Gregorian Chant 440 Hz.)
Let nothing break this covenant. By our blood we seal it. It is finished.

SEMJAZA
It is finished.

DISSOLVE TO:

INT. ENOCH'S HUT - NIGHT

Enoch finishes writing text above and proceeds to write text below, dipping his quill in ink after each letter.

ENOCH (V.O.)
And they were in all two hundred; who descended in the days of Jared on the summit of Mount Hermon, and they called it Mount Hermon, because they had sworn and bound themselves by mutual imprecations upon it. And they took wives from the daughters of earth for themselves.

QUICK SHOTS

WOMAN'S eyes adorned with makeup behind a veil.

WOMAN'S lips visible through the veil.

The Veil is pulled off by man's arm as Woman runs away.

Her arm is grabbed by a firm hand as she tries to run from him.

CUT TO BLACK:

EXT. GRAVE SITE - NIGHT

Sister holds baby Na'eltama'uk fireside.

Mother's body is wrapped in linen, adorned with greenery and flowers.

Great MEN OF OLD chant along with Armaros, Azazel and his son young Aviv.

ENOCH (V.O.)
Some of the mortal bodies of women could not withstand the great power these children possessed.

Young Aviv lights colored smoke/incense with a torch. Smoke travels into the night sky and colors combine together.

Chanting and meditating continues.

Na'eltama'uk shifts within Sister's arms and gurgles.

ENOCH (V.O.)
Their children were called the Nephilim.

Chanting and meditating continues.

MATCH CUT TO:

EXT. FIELD - NIGHT

MONTAGE OF THE FALLEN ANGEL TEACHERS

Armaros, Sister and YOUNG NA'ELTAMA'UK (toddler age) are seated in a circle.

PUNGI PLAYER plays his instrument (pungi) in a meditative posture.

Mouth chanting echoes in the air.

ALL
(chanting)
Shama...Shama.

ENOCH (V.O.)
Wives, their children learned a variety of new skills from the fallen...Sorcery, spells and technological advances.

AMAROS
(chanting)
Nachash...Nachash...Nachash.

ENOCH (V.O.)
Armaros taught the resolving of inner conflict and ways of the serpent.

A snake comes into view. It sits in front of Na'eltama'uk.

YOUNG NA'ELTAMA'UK & SISTER
(singing, in Hebrew)
Hush my sweet serpent, hear my sweet call. Lead forth your children from cave to my shawl.

Snake is quickly hypnotized by music.

YOUNG NA'ELTAMA'UK & SISTER (CONT'D)
(singing, in Hebrew)
No pain will come to your shining scaled brood. I sing you to sleep in your sanctuary wood.

JUMP CUT:

EXT. STARRY SKY - NIGHT

We see BARAQIJAL and KOKABIEL with their arms outstretched over backdrop of stars. An astrology diagram lights up in night sky over a awestruck CROWD.

KOKABIEL
It is written in the stars, that mankind must submit to the sons of God.

ENOCH (V.O.)
Baraqijal taught astrology. Kokabiel used the knowledge of the constellations to force his will upon mankind and ideas of the future.

KOKABIEL
I have come to you, to bring knowledge. You are a people lost in the struggles of humanity. You forget the harmony that exists in the cosmos. Look up at the stars!

The crowd lifts their gaze towards a night sky, including Young Aviv.

KOKABIEL (CONT'D)
In them are reflections of your past and what's to come. Do not ignore their call.

Baraqijal steps forward.

BARAQIJAL
Every star holds the energy of the cosmos. The father kept these secrets from you to cause confusion. We have come to give you knowledge and understanding so you can be like Him.

Some in the crowd nod and lean in, heavily engaged.

Young Aviv looks determined and ready to unlock great mysteries.

BARAQIJAL (CONT'D)
Young boy!

Aviv quickly stands to his feet.

BARAQIJAL (CONT'D)
It is written in the stars that you will be a great warrior.

Baraqijal takes red clay from the earth and wipes it on Aviv's face. His father, Azazel, smiles proudly in the distance.

BARAQIJAL (CONT'D)
May nothing stand in the way of your great call.

DISSOLVE TO:

INT. CLASSROOM HUT - DAY

PENEMUEL writes Hebrew alphabet on a rock to young children who practice writing their names.

ENOCH (V.O.)
Penemuel brought written language to the people. Penemuel used the written word to manipulate and control man.

Na'eltama'uk's (Aged 6) rock has her name written a few times but is covered in distracting drawings of a snake and a girl.

Penemuel takes her writing utensil and continues to move about the room.

CUT TO:

EXT. VILLAGE - DAY

SUNSET.

SEMJAZA, draped in black silk, gathers roots from ground and places it in a bowl of purple smoke.

ENOCH (V.O.)
Semjaza taught enchantments, and root-cuttings to engage with the demonic.

A tribe encircles Aviv (16). He has clay markings on his face.

SEMJAZA
Ziwa, Ajna! Ziwa, Ajna!

They dance around him, throwing black ash on him in a ceremony of manhood.

ALL
Ziwa, Ajna! Ziwa, Ajna!

His father Azazel smiles proudly for his son and places war paint on his face.

AZAZEL
You are ready my son.

JUMP CUT:

EXT. FIRE PIT - DAY

Aviv forges a sword in the fire under direction of his father Azazel.

ENOCH (V.O.)
Azazel taught weaponry and war.

The two begin to hammer on anvil to shape the sword.

AZAZEL
More pressure Aviv.

Aviv hammers harder.

AZAZEL (CONT'D)
More!

Aviv hammers with more intensity.

AZAZEL (CONT'D)
Good.

EXT. COOLING/SHARPENING STATION - DAY

Azazel and Aviv craft a hilt and handle for their sword.

Azazel's wraps leather around the handle and ties it. Aviv's hands follow his lead.

AZAZEL
You will fight for the bloodline of our people. Let nothing stand in your way.

TEEN AVIV
Yes father.

Aviv sharpens the blade of his sword while watching Azazel sharpen his.

AZAZEL
Man is but flesh and bone. You my son, are superior.

EXT. NEARBY FIELD - DAY

Aviv tries out his new sword, swinging it through the air with war hungry eyes.

AZAZEL
Give me more!

Aviv gives more energy and continues to swing his sword.

AZAZEL (CONT'D)
More!

ENOCH (V.O.)
Azazel wanted war... Suffering for mankind to pit them against one another.

Azazel continues to yell at his son as the sound drops to a mute.

Aviv tries different sword combinations, looking hopefully at Azazel between each attempt.

ENOCH (V.O.)
And against their God.

Continued muted yelling of Azazel at his son.

DISSOLVE TO:

EXT. FIELD - DAY

Azazel and Aviv make arrow heads and a bow.

ENOCH (V.O.)
To corrupt the bloodline of major tribes and families to prevent the vessel from which a messiah would be born.

In the distance, is a helpless sheep.

AZAZEL
There. By the bush. Aim...

Azazel helps position Aviv's arms.

AZAZEL (CONT'D)
Focus on the target. When you have your shot, shoot. And shoot to kill.

Aviv lines up with the sheep. He pulls back to release arrow but second guesses himself.

AZAZEL (CONT'D)
Why do you hesitate?!

Azazel positions his hands over his sons and speaks in his ear.

AZAZEL (CONT'D)
Get out of your own way!

Azazel pulls back his sons hand to shoot bow for him.

AZAZEL (CONT'D)
War is not a game of the mind and heart. You must quiet them both.

The sheep helplessly stands there. The arrow flies through air. The sound of a hit/dying animal is heard.

Azazel hands over a knife to Aviv.

AZAZEL (CONT'D)
Finish it!

Aviv peers intensely at the knife.

AVIV
Yes father.

Aviv goes to finish his kill. He raises his knife, trembling hands.

MATCH CUT:

EXT. FIELD - DAY

TIME JUMP

As his hands come down, they are grown hands. He is older and wiser (AVIV late 20s, very large man).

He prepares the meat from his kill.

Azazel approaches. Aviv looks over. Azazel is stoic and gives a nod that Aviv clearly understands.

DISSOLVE TO:

EXT. BATTLE FIELD - DAY

Na'eltama'uk (14 yrs) gathers lavender in a field to put it into a cloth doll.

She sees WARRIORS preparing for battle and runs back home with her doll.

Aviv is one of many men preparing for war alongside his father Azazel who addresses the Warriors.

AZAZEL
Today we fight for power! We fight for honor! And the bloodline of our people! Today we write our saga in sweat and blood! Let the cries of our enemy be our song!

Men raise their weapons to the sky. The Fallen in black silk ride on black horses behind the warriors.

ALL WARRIORS & FALLEN ANGELS
Ay!

AZAZEL
We fight as one!
(pause)
Not for a heavenly god but for the SONS OF GOD!

SE'IRIM (goat-demons) and a GIANT walk alongside the army.

AZAZEL (CONT'D)
Let's finish it!

ALL WARRIORS & FALLEN ANGELS
Ay!

Aviv leads the army with confidence. Battle ensues.

A large GIANT fights alongside Azazel. Giant grabs opposing men and throws them in air.

Swords clash. Demon goats charge enemy lines.

A few of the Fallen in black silk are thrown from their horses by a large giant.

They beam themselves out of the fight. A few stay and fight, including Semjaza.

Giant blows fire on half of Azazel's army. Semjaza, Azazel, Aviv and a few others barely escape the flames.

Village is ransacked by enemy. Sounds of children and women screaming/crying is heard as they run from burning huts.

INT./EXT. SMALL HUT - DAY

Sister hides Na'eltama'uk behind linen. Sister hands her a curved sword.

SISTER
Take it. Use it if you need it.

NA'ELTAMA'UK
Where are you going?!

SISTER
Stay here...

NA'ELTAMA'UK
I want to stay with you.

SISTER
Na'eltama'uk! Do as I say.

NA'ELTAMA'UK
But I can help.

SISTER
No. You can't.

She covers Na'eltama'uk. A GIANT MAN from opposing side barges into the hut. He corners Sister.

SISTER (CONT'D)
I will go with you quietly. Don't kill me.

Giant man holds her by the neck. He looks at her body with lust.

P.O.V - Na'eltama'uk's eyes under sheet watch Sister with Giant Man.

SISTER (CONT'D)
Whatever you want I will give it to you. Just spare my life, please.

Giant man pushes sister's body up against a wall.

EXT. FIELD - DAY

Aviv runs confidently into battle breaking 4th wall. He runs/climbs on the backs of his army and leaps into air, piercing monstrous giant.

Semjaza and Azazel rush the enemy. Swords continue to clash around them.

Slow motion fighting over voice over dialogue.

ENOCH (V.O.)
War, greed, lust. Suffocating the breath of humanity... In order to restore balance, God sent down his archangels.

A great light descends from the sky.

ENOCH (V.O.)
...To purge the evil and bring warning of what was to come.

Archangel RAPHAEL appears to Azazel. Azazel lifts his chest and raises his sword for battle.

RAPHAEL
You bring dishonor to your God and corruption upon this land!

Azazel's black wings emerge.

AZAZEL
He is not my God!... I am my own god!

Raphael pulls out a sword of fire.

Azazel slashes, Raphael parries. Azazel blocks countermove and thrusts his weapon forward.

Raphael blocks and parries. Azazel ripostes.

RAPHAEL
Repent and come back to God!
Surrender your heart to Him.

Azazel laughs.

AZAZEL
Surrender?! I will not!

Azazel slashes forward. Raphael parries and knocks Azazel to the ground. Chains of blue fire bind Azazel's hands and feet.

RAPHAEL
You will be bound to the desert
rocks of Dudael!

Aviv sees his father bound from a distance. Semjaza is knocked to the ground and the enemy has a sword at his neck.

To cheat death, Semjaza beams himself out of the situation.

AVIV
Father!

Aviv runs toward his father, killing opposing men along the way.

Azazel uses his sword of red fire to try and break chains of blue fire.

Azazel cannot cut through chains of blue fire. He sinks into the rocks and becomes stone, leaving his sword behind.

Raphael disappears.

Aviv runs toward rock where his father was.

AVIV (CONT'D)
Father!!

Aviv places his hands upon rock and cries out again.

AVIV (CONT'D)
Father!

Aviv hangs his head in sorrow on rock form of his father.

AVIV (CONT'D)
(under breath)
I have failed you. Forgive me.

CUT TO:

INT. ENOCH'S HUT/KITCHEN - DAY

Enoch puts down his writing quill, his eyes full of emotion.

He gets up and washes his hands in a bowl of water seven times.

On the seventh time, he puts water on his face. He drys his hands and face with a nearby cloth.

Enoch bows his head in prayer.

ENOCH
God. Be with me.

He pulls out a piece of animal skin from a wooden bucket of water and salt.

He rings it out and begins to remove hair from animal skin with a special tool.

Pieces of dry parchment paper hang in the background.

ENOCH (CONT'D)
Let my heart, my hands be steadfast
on serving you oh Lord.

Animal hair falls to the ground.

He squeezes lime into the bucket of water. He lays animal skin back in water to continue processing.

He walks back to the wash bowl and washes his hands seven times before returning to his desk/table.

He picks up his writing quill and continues to write.

Words are narrated as he writes text.

ENOCH (V.O.)
But ye. Ye have not been steadfast,
nor done the commandments of the
Lord but ye have turned away and
spoken proud-

CUT TO:

EXT. DESOLATE FIELD - DAY

Aviv walks through bodies of dead soldiers including Armaros's dying body (Na'eltama'uk's dad).

Armaros's eyes are open. He coughs up blood as he tries to get off the ground. Aviv takes his hand.

ARMAROS
Na'eltam'uk. See to her...

Armaros dies.

Aviv gently brushes his fingers on Armaros's eyelids to close them.

AVIV
Armaros. Go in peace.
(whispers)
I am sorry.
(pause)
I swear on my very breath that I will bring vengeance on anyone who comes against us... I will carry out the plan... You have my word.

CUT TO:

EXT. DESOLATE FIELD/VILLAGE - DAY

Aviv walks through what is left of his village and gathers himself. He hears the sound of a young girl crying from a small hut and stops.

Aviv looks into the hut.

INT/EXT. SMALL HUT - DAY

Na'eltama'uk is crying beneath the blanket. She sees Aviv's feet walk in through the blanket and sits still and silent.

Aviv steps over Aunt's dead body in the doorway, her clothes noticeably ripped.

He steps over a pierced enemy who is barely alive to get to Na'eltama'uk. He pulls the blanket off her face.

NA'ELTAMA'UK
Get back!

Na'eltama'uk holds up the sword Aunt gave her with remnants of blood on the blade and her hands.

AVIV
I won't hurt you.

Na'eltama'uk's hands shake. Her doll made of cloth, yarn and sand lays on her lap.

NA'ELTAMA'UK
I said get back!

Aviv steps back and looks at her face.

AVIV
You are the daughter of Armaros...
Our Fathers' were friends.

NA'ELTAMA'UK
Where is my father? He said he
would come back for me.

Aviv hesitates.

NA'ELTAMA'UK (CONT'D)
Where is he!?

AVIV
Your father is no more and mine
with him... I tell you the truth.

Na'eltama'uk interrupts, still pointing her sword at Aviv.

NA'ELTAMA'UK
I don't believe you.

AVIV
I wish it wasn't true. Please, put
down your sword.

NA'ELTAMA'UK
No

AVIV
You should come with me. It's not
safe for you here.

NA'ELTAMA'UK
How can I trust that you are safe?

Giant Man in the background tries to get up despite his deep wound.

NA'ELTAMA'UK (CONT'D)
I will stay here and wait for my
father.

AVIV
I told you, your father is no
more...

NA'ELTAMA'UK
I will believe it when I see for myself!

Aviv looks back at the body of Sister.

AVIV
Is this your mother?

NA'ELTAMA'UK
My mother died when I was born. She was my Aunt but raised me as her own... This man took what he wanted from her and then killed her. So I pierced him with this sword.

Aviv walks over to Giant Man struggling.

He hovers over him as he tries to reach for his weapon.

AVIV
Where are your men to save you?

GIANT MAN
I call upon the spirits of the dead to bring forth misfortune on your people!

Aviv gets in his face. Giant man spits in Aviv's face and laughs with evil intent in his eyes.

GIANT MAN (CONT'D)
(chanting)
Go n-ithe an cat thu, is go n-ithe an diabhal an cat!

Aviv finishes him. Na'eltama'uk is scared but relieved.

AVIV
It is not safe for you here.

Na'eltama'uk hesitates.

NA'ELTAMA'UK
I will go with you... I want to see my father... Before we go.

EXT. DESOLATE FIELD - DAY

Na'eltama'uk kneels by her dead father. She takes out her oils and anoints his forehead.

NA'ELTAMA'UK
Father.

Na'eltama'uk unties the leather strap necklace with stone from around her father's neck (identical necklace to MOHAMMAD THE WOLF'S MOM).

She wraps it around her handmade doll's waist a few times to make a belt. She places her hand on her father's heart.

Aviv grabs the sword of Armaros and breaks it. He gives the pieces to Na'eltama'uk.

She digs a hole in the ground and places the sword pieces down in it.

Longer beat.

She covers sword pieces with sand.

NA'ELTAMA'UK (CONT'D)
I have no one left now.

AVIV
Your father would have wanted me to watch over you. I vow to keep you safe... I give you my word.

Aviv puts out his hand to pull her up. She doesn't take it and pulls herself up.

CU on doll's smile in Na'eltama'uk's satchel.

MATCH CUT TO:

EXT. FOREST - DAY

CU of the doll's smile sticking out of a leather satchel as Na'eltama'uk walks.

Aviv leads her through a wooded area.

CU on feet walking through heavy terrain.

AVIV
What's with the doll anyway? Aren't you a little too old to be playing with dolls?

NA'ELTAMA'UK
She was made from the garments of my mother.
(MORE)

NA'ELTAMA'UK (CONT'D)
It's really all I have from her. And now, all I have left of my father.

CU on doll's belt (Father's necklace).

AVIV
Shouldn't you be preparing for your betrothal?

NA'ELTAMA'UK
Where is your wife?... So quick to marry me off, what about you?

AVIV
My wife died along with our first child.

NA'ELTAMA'UK
Oh.

AVIV
No time to sit and wallow over what is no more.

Aviv cuts through a path as they walk.

NA'ELTAMA'UK
I think it's okay to think about them... Do you ever wonder where they went or what they're doing?

AVIV
I reserve my thoughts for more productive things.

NA'ELTAMA'UK
Thoughts and memories can be productive.

AVIV
They can also be a quicksand. Trust me.

Aviv continues to cut through paths as they walk.

NA'ELTAMA'UK
Where exactly are we going?

AVIV
We are going to the sorcerer. She will show us the way.

Aviv and Na'eltama'uk continue to walk through wooded terrain.

NA'ELTAMA'UK
I hope she tells us to get food.

AVIV
We will eat after dusk. We cannot waste the daylight.

NA'ELTAMA'UK
I don't know if I can wait that long.

Aviv pulls a few berries off a nearby bush.

AVIV
Here...

NA'ELTAMA'UK
What am I supposed to do with three berries?!

AVIV
Eat them.

Aviv continues to walk.

Na'eltama'uk looks down at three berries.

Longer beat.

She sighs and pops them into her mouth.

They continue to walk. Na'eltama'uk runs to catch up. She looks at Aviv's bags of weapons with judgement.

NA'ELTAMA'UK
Do you ever wonder if the world would be better without war?

AVIV
War is necessary.

NA'ELTAMA'UK
I hate it.

AVIV
Your father fought to protect many. My father did too. There is no greater feat than to fight for power and for freedom... You'll understand when you're older.

The two continue to walk.

NA'ELTAMA'UK
I don't know that I want to.
I prefer peace. Meditation. Oils.

AVIV
Meditation won't save you when
there is a sword against your back.
Neither will oils.

They continue to walk, Aviv cuts down branches in the way.

AVIV (CONT'D)
The bloodline of our people is at
stake. We cannot back down now. Our
fathers will not die in vain.

CUT TO:

EXT. NOAH'S BUILDING AREA - NIGHT

NOAH works diligently on what appears to be something large. It is 70 percent done. Others in family work in background. CU on Noah's hands working.

HAM
Father is this not crazy?

Noah stops hammering with a wooden mallet.

HAM (CONT'D)
There has to be another way. Could
you not go to the Lord and ask him?
If He destroys these lands what
will we build on?

NOAH
We must have faith.

Noah takes a drink of his water, continues hammering.

NOAH (CONT'D)
As the day approaches it will only
get harder to keep the faith.
Trust God in this. He has made a
way for us.

A BLACK SILK ANGEL spies on Noah's camp in the distance.

DISSOLVE TO:

EXT. ANCIENT MEETING SPACE MT. HERMON - NIGHT

A small group of Fallen Angels are gathered adorned in their black silk. Tensions are high.

Semjaza stands at the head of table, addressing the others. His expression is stern.

SEMJAZA
(commanding)
Cowardly!

The others look down in embarrassment. FALLEN SKEPTIC looks concerned.

SEMJAZA (CONT'D)
I fought alone, and where were all of you?!

FALLEN SKEPTIC
We had no chance against an army of that size.

Semjaza's eyes narrow, his grip tightening on the edge of the table. He flips the table and the Fallen Angels back away from it.

SEMJAZA
Traitor! Have you forgotten the oath you swore?! THE COVENANT WE SEALED IN BLOOD?!

FALLEN SKEPTIC
If we continue we will surely perish and pay for our transgressions.

SEMJAZA
Then we will pay whatever the cost!

Fallen Skeptic's cloak turns from black to grey. Semjaza picks him up by the neckline of his cloak.

SEMJAZA (CONT'D)
You. You're lukewarm.

He throws him to the ground. Fallen Skeptic rises, his cloak has turned an even lighter grey.

Semjaza draws his sword. Fallen Skeptic draws his. Fallen Skeptic fights with desperation, his blade a blur as he tries to fend off the onslaught.

Semjaza's forces are too many. Fallen Skeptic's defenses crumble.

Fallen Skeptic pushes back one final time, knocking Semjaza to the ground, Fallen Skeptic's sword held to his neck.

FALLEN SKEPTIC
I want no part of this.

He removes sword from Semjaza's neck. As he exits his cloak turns to white. Semjaza pierces him in the back.

Fallen Skeptic falls to the ground. Semjaza turns to address the others.

SEMJAZA
Anyone else want to go against me?!

The men hang their heads in fear.

Fallen Skeptic crawls toward exit of cave.

FALLEN SKEPTIC
(under breath)
Father forgive me.

Semjaza kills him.

FADE TO:

EXT. SORCERER CAVE - DUSK

Na'eltama'uk and Aviv approach a cave entrance.

As they approach cave entrance, Aviv encounters a seemingly harmless cloud of shimmering, iridescent bugs swirling in the air.

Aviv swats them away.

NA'ELTAMA'UK
I wouldn't do that if I were you.

Aviv continues to swat at the bugs. They emit a mist of dangerous toxins in the air. Na'eltama'uk remains distant.

Aviv continues to swat at them with his sword, more dangerous mist emitted into the air.

Aviv passes out.

NA'ELTAMA'UK (CONT'D)
I warned you.

DISSOLVE TO:

EXT. SORCERER CAVE - DUSK

Fire with colored incense burns on corners of a wooden table.

Aviv lies in the corner, resting off his toxic encounter. Na'eltama'uk puts oils on his temples.

He shoots up from triggering smell.

NA'ELTAMA'UK
Your sword was no match for the Hazewing Sprites.

The head of a SORCERER sits on a table attached to an old embellished plate.

Sorcerer's eyes open.

SORCERER
Nice of you to join us, Aviv.

SORCERER (CONT'D)
Come closer.

Aviv moves in, hesitant.

SORCERER (CONT'D)
I don't bite. And neither do the bugs. They're harmless really if left alone.

AVIV
They were in my way.

SORCERER
Maybe you were in their way.

Aviv clears his voice.

AVIV
Great sorcerer... We seek your wisdom on where to go from here. Our homeland has been destroyed along with our people... I have no army. But my heart wants war... justice for my father. And for hers.

SORCERER
I see.

AVIV
We must fight to keep our bloodline alive.

SORCERER
Your bloodline... Yes... And what if I told you, you don't need an army to fight this battle.

AVIV
I don't understand, no army? We will surely die.

SORCERER
There is the physical war and then there is the unseen war. You must focus on what is unseen.

Sorcerer closes her eyes and takes a deep breath.

Longer beat.

SORCERER (CONT'D)
There is something coming that weapons cannot stand against. No it's not bugs.

AVIV
What is coming?

SORCERER
Great judgement.

Na'eltama'uk listens intently to sorcerer.

SORCERER (CONT'D)
And everything we see and know will be destroyed.

AVIV
I will stop it.

SORCERER
You cannot stop this.

Sorcerer's eyes open.

SORCERER (CONT'D)
You must find the one who builds from the trees of the forest.
(MORE)

SORCERER (CONT'D)
His instructions come from the mouth of God. He is building something.

AVIV
I will not help this man or his god! God has done nothing for me. Why would I do anything for him?

Sorcerer's eyes turn red. Fire blazes from sides of table and her voice intensifies with triple voices.

SORCERER
You ask me the way but go your own?!

Aviv cowers.

Na'eltama'uk hides behind Aviv, frightened.

SORCERER (CONT'D)
This will not serve you well Aviv. Mark my words, if you don't turn from your pride, you will die by it and the chains of your resentment will sink your body into the deep! Just like your father.

Aviv lifts his head for a moment.

AVIV
My father was a good man.

SORCERER
Good?

AVIV
He fought for his people, is that not good?!

Flames on the corner of the table blaze again.

SORCERER
You know little of what is good.

Aviv turns from her intensity.

SORCERER (CONT'D)
You don't want what is good. You just WANT.

AVIV
What I want is justice for my father.

SORCERER
Are you sure it's justice you seek and not his approval?

He looks down to distract from her truth.

SORCERER (CONT'D)
Oh the weight of a father's judgement. I can see it on you now.

Sorcerer closes her eyes.

SORCERER (CONT'D)
A body without it's heart is dead.

Sorcerer opens her eyes.

SORCERER (CONT'D)
A boat without direction is driftwood. You must learn to lean into your heart and fully feel things.

AVIV
There is no time to feel, only to act. That is why we came to see you... For direction.

SORCERER
You came to me to affirm what you already had planned. I am telling you there is a better way.

AVIV
I only know the ways of war.

SORCERER
Your victory is not found in what you know, but what you will learn. Find the builder, then you will understand.

Na'eltama'uk peers out from behind Aviv.

SORCERER (CONT'D)
And you.

Sorcerer looks into the eyes of Na'eltama'uk.

SORCERER (CONT'D)
Na'eltama'uk, come.

Na'eltama'uk walks slowly to her.

SORCERER (CONT'D)
You have many gifts my child. The blood of the gods, but the heart of mortals. Your path will be the conduit for your bloodline. But be mindful of your dreams and visions. They can serve as a light for your path or a prison for your soul.

Sorcerer looks at Aviv, then nods to Na'eltama'uk.

SORCERER (CONT'D)
Follow the belt of Orion, past desert lands. You will find him where the sand turns fertile... Since you came with barely nothing, I have put together some essentials for your trip... There. By the door.

Na'eltama'uk walks toward the door and sees two leather woven backpacks packed for their trip; one small, one large.

Na'eltama'uk opens it and sees a small blanket and pillow for her doll, among other essentials.

NA'ELTAMA'UK
For my doll.

Sorcerer smiles.

Na'eltama'uk places her doll in a special compartment on outside of her bag. Aviv picks up his bag and looks back at sorcerer.

AVIV
We shall be on our way then.

SORCERER
Shalom aleichem.

NA'ELTAMA'UK
Thank you.

CUT TO:

EXT. NOAH'S BUILDING AREA - NIGHT

Noah chops hay and prepares it in baskets.

NOAH'S WIFE
It's late. Come to bed.

NOAH
Just a few more.

NOAH'S WIFE
Can we talk about our son for a moment?

Noah continues to chop hay and section it out.

NOAH
What is there to talk about?

NOAH'S WIFE
A suitable wife. I'm afraid this journey will be quite lonely for him. And how can he be in obedience to God to repopulate the earth without a companion?

NOAH
God will provide.

NOAH'S WIFE
I could go into town and see.

NOAH
God will provide, we need not intervene.

He sections off more hay.

NOAH'S WIFE
I understand.

Noah pours water into basins.

DISSOLVE TO:

EXT. WATERS OF DAN - NIGHT

Enoch is asleep on shoreline. Water rushes over him. The water quickly becomes clouds. A heavy mist carries him into sky full of stars.

EXT. THE HEAVENS - NIGHT

DREAM

Enoch sees walls of crystals surrounded by angels singing.

Fire comes from their mouths with each note. Enoch is frightened but continues to walk forward.

As he continues to walk, each step is crystalized under a pool of water.

To his right are circular portals of fire and to the left.

As he enters, he falls to his knees. ANGEL OF LIGHT with light brighter than snow surrounds Enoch.

ANGEL OF LIGHT
Fear not, Enoch, thou noble man and scribe of righteousness. Approach hither and hear my voice.

ENOCH
Has the Father heard my plea for his angels and his people? I have come to see if there is a way to save them.

ANGEL OF LIGHT
He has given countless warnings to the sons of God and they have chosen lust, pride and war. Even in your warning they have still gone back to what is evil. Their wives and children have also chosen evil... You must warn them of their trespasses and what is to come.

Great winds hit Enoch from all sides.

ANGEL OF LIGHT (CONT'D)
Come with me.

Enoch proceeds forward. He sees a magnificent place that burns day and night.

In the distance, there are seven mountains with different colored stones; one of pearl, one of jacinth, some were red stone.

In the middle, a stone reaches to incredible heights. It is made of sapphire.

Beautiful birds fly and they sing heavenly songs.

ANGEL OF LIGHT (CONT'D)
They will not be with us here.

Enoch is beamed forward to a horrible place where columns of fire fall all around him.

There are no birds flying and music/cries are disturbing to hear.

Enoch reaches for what looks like a hurt dove on the ground. As he picks it up, pieces of it turn to ash/sand.

DREAM ENDS

MATCH CUT TO:

EXT. WATERS OF DAN - NIGHT

Enoch sits on the shoreline with hands full of sand. He bows his head as water continues to rush over him.

DISSOLVE TO:

EXT. FOREST - FIRESIDE - NIGHT

Aviv positions brittle pieces of tinder for fire.

NA'ELTAMA'UK
Is this when we eat?

Aviv blows on fire, ignoring Na'eltama'uk.

NA'ELTAMA'UK (CONT'D)
I could gather berries or greens. Flowers for oils?

Aviv continues to tend to the fire. Na'eltama'uk smells a piece of lavender she pulls from the ground.

NA'ELTAMA'UK (CONT'D)
I love the smell of lavender don't you? I put lavender in my doll.

She holds doll up for him to smell.

NA'ELTAMA'UK (CONT'D)
You want to smell her?

Aviv pushes the doll away.

AVIV
I don't like the smell of lavender.

NA'ELTAMA'UK
What's wrong with lavender?

Aviv blows on the fire to help it grow, ignoring her.

Na'eltama'uk plays with her doll.

NA'ELTAMA'UK (CONT'D)
What did you play with when you were a kid?

AVIV
I didn't play.

NA'ELTAMA'UK
You never made a crown and pretended to be king? Or caught dragons with people made of paper?

AVIV
What's the point of imaginary war? There's too many battles to be fought in real life.

Aviv places more wood around the fire.

AVIV (CONT'D)
I was 9 when I killed a man. The earthly grew fearful of our knowledge and saw us as a threat to their power and to their women. They ransacked our village in the middle of the night. I sent my sword through a man's stomach.

His demeanor quickly changes to pride. Na'eltama'uk lays fireside looking up to the sky, holding her doll to her stomach.

AVIV (CONT'D)
You do what you have to do.

Aviv laces up his sandals.

NA'ELTAMA'UK
Is it ever enough though? We pierce one another in the name of peace but go back to our grief and anger the next second. For what?

AVIV
You think too much. And you ask too many questions.

Aviv gathers his bow and arrow. Na'eltama'uk continues to hold tightly to her doll.

Aviv puts on his satchel.

AVIV (CONT'D)
You stay here. Keep watch.

NA'ELTAMA'UK
Where are you going?

Aviv holds up his bow.

AVIV
Do you want food or not?

CUT TO:

EXT. FOREST - NIGHT

Aviv travels carefully into the forest. He stops at a tree and gathers a few pieces of fruit and places it in his bag.

He hears something in the trees to his right and quickly gets out his arrow and points it that way.

He continues to walk forward. He hears something in the trees to his left and quickly points arrow left.

He sees a rabbit and points his arrow.

He shoots and hits it. He pridefully smiles.

EXT. FOREST - FIRESIDE - NIGHT

Na'eltama'uk continues to lay on her back. She holds her doll up to sky and brings it into her chest.

She raises her hand to the sky to measure the stars. Her stomach growls.

Na'eltama'uk gets up and wanders into a wooded area of dying trees, doll securely in her bag.

EXT. DYING FOREST - NIGHT

She pulls an unknown fruit from a tree and stares at it.

She breaks fruit open.

The ground beneath her starts to shake and rises up. She fearfully crouches down as her body rises up past the trees.

HUBRIS (a 20 foot Tree Monster) rises from the ground. His arms are many; They are functional tree branches. He roars loudly.

EXT. FOREST - NIGHT

The ground shakes beneath Aviv and he hears a mighty roar. He stumbles to the ground, dropping food collected.

He quickly gathers items dropped, places them in his bag and rushes back to camp site.

AVIV
(under breath)
Na'eltama'uk...

He hears another roar and runs faster.

EXT. DYING FOREST - NIGHT

Na'eltama'uk holds tightly to the top of Hubris. He looks around but sees no one. Hubris snarls in frustration.

Hubris looks down and sees Na'eltama'uk's doll. He picks up the doll and as he bends down, Na'eltama'uk falls off.

Na'eltama'uk trembles and quickly scoots away from Hubris.

NA'ELTAMA'UK
We mean you no harm!

He roars loudly.

HUBRIS
We?!

He snarls.

HUBRIS (CONT'D)
There arc more of you?!

He coughs and tries to catch his breath.

HUBRIS (CONT'D)
How many are there?!

Hubris grabs Na'eltama'uk and holds her tightly. He roars in her face.

NA'ELTAMA'UK
The man I am traveling with. He went to find food. It's just us. I promise you. There are no more.

He smells her. He coughs again and struggles to breathe.

NA'ELTAMA'UK (CONT'D)
What is your name?

Hubris hesitates and snarls. Na'eltama'uk puts hand on her heart.

NA'ELTAMA'UK (CONT'D)
Na'eltama'uk. My name is Na'eltama'uk... What's yours?

Hubris pulls back his growl.

NA'ELTAMA'UK (CONT'D)
I won't hurt you.

Hubris hesitates.

TREE MONSTER
Hubris.

NA'ELTAMA'UK
Hubris. I like that name... I can help you, Hubris. With your cough.

Hubris loosens his grip with a small glimpse of trust.

Na'eltama'uk gets lavender oil from her bag and places it near the nostrils of Hubris.

NA'ELTAMA'UK (CONT'D)
Breathe in.

He turns his head away.

NA'ELTAMA'UK (CONT'D)
I promise, it will help you.

He hesitates but turns his head toward her. He takes a deep breath in.

Aviv shoots an arrow into the side of Hubris O/S. Hubris drops Na'eltama'uk and her doll. He growls in anger/pain.

Na'eltama'uk grabs her doll.

AVIV
Run Na'eltama'uk!

Hubris stands to his feet. Na'eltama'uk runs to Aviv with her hand out to stop him. Aviv shoots another arrow into Hubris.

NA'ELTAMA'UK
Stop!

Hubris falls to the ground. Aviv grabs another arrow to shoot again. He pulls back string of his bow.

NA'ELTAMA'UK (CONT'D)
Don't shoot him! Please!

Na'eltama'uk stands in front of Aviv.

AVIV
Move!

NA'ELTAMA'UK
Don't shoot.

Hubris struggles to get up in background.

AVIV
And why not?! He will surely kill us.

NA'ELTAMA'UK
He needs water. The land is too dry.

Aviv aims to shoot again.

NA'ELTAMA'UK (CONT'D)
He's dying.

Hubris coughs and struggles to breathe in background.

AVIV
He will kill us.

NA'ELTAMA'UK
He can help us.

AVIV
I don't want his help.

Aviv aims to shoot again. Na'eltama'uk puts her hand on bow.

AVIV (CONT'D)
He is no help to me half dead.

NA'ELTAMA'UK
Maybe some food will help him regain his strength.

Aviv sighs and puts down his bow.

AVI
So I'm taking orders from a child now?

He walks away.

NA'ELTAMA'UK
I'm not a child.

AVIV
You're gonna' get us both killed. This isn't some paper dragon. You know nothing about this beast and what he is capable of.

CUT TO:

EXT. FOREST - FIRESIDE - NIGHT

Na'eltama'uk tends to Hubris's wounds as he drinks water.

Aviv prepares food over fire.

HUBRIS
Thank you. For the water.

NA'ELTAMA'UK
You're welcome.

Aviv pours three soups into misshapen wooden bowls.

AVIV
It's not much, but at least it's something to eat.

Na'eltama'uk takes her soup. Aviv then offers Hubris a soup bowl.

AVIV (CONT'D)
Here...

Hubris turns his head away.

AVIV (CONT'D)
You're not going to let me trying to kill you earlier get in the way of a good meal, are you?

Hubris looks at soup out of corner of his eye.

AVIV (CONT'D)
Come on.

Hubris takes soup and drinks it.

As he drinks, life comes back into his branches and a few leaves start to grow.

AVIV (CONT'D)
We must journey at surrise. This land is cursed. There is barely any food.

Aviv ponders a beat and looks over to Hubris

AVIV (CONT'D)
Why would you stay here?

Na'eltama'uk finishes her soup. She lays her head down and closes her eyes in background.

HUBRIS
When I wanted to leave, my roots were too weak to go. I prayed for rain but the creator was silent with me. I prayed for the company of birds but there has been no song.

DISSOLVE TO:

FLASHBACK

Hubris and family are tied up by SONS OF GOD, EVIL MEN.

HUBRIS (V.O.)
The sons of god and mankind enslaved my brothers to fight their wars. My family...

AN EVIL MAN'S sword slashes down breaking 4th wall.

HUBRIS (V.O.)
Cut down and used for weaponry.

Pieces a wood carried by WARRIORS while OTHERS shape wood into weaponry.

FLASHBACK ENDS

HUBRIS
In my anger I devoured an entire village. I thought it would satisfy me.

(MORE)

HUBRIS (CONT'D)
But nothing could satisfy my grief. I mourned my family here. I grieved my sin. And as I cried, life left me withered and empty.

He takes a drink of soup.

HUBRIS (CONT'D)
Maybe the God of the universe sent you to test me. To see if my anger still steers me.

AVIV
It sounds like this God has abandoned you.

HUBRIS
I abandoned him... I need to speak with him again.

Aviv chuckles.

AVIV
Any god who ignores his creation is not a god but a coward.

HUBRIS
I have done detestable things, yet he was still patient with me. Odious things... I long to hear his voice again.

AVIV
The man we are traveling to find, speaks with this God. Maybe he can tell you why he has left you to die.

Aviv pauses a moment.

AVIV (CONT'D)
But if you go, I cannot carry the weight of your weakness.

Aviv sees Na'eltama'uk is asleep.

AVIV (CONT'D)
The girl is enough trouble as it is.

Aviv covers her with her blanket. He prepares his bed for sleep.

HUBRIS
If I become a burden I will excuse myself. I owe her a debt for saving my life.

Hubris looks at Na'eltama'uk, sound asleep.

HUBRIS (CONT'D)
You on the other hand.

AVIV
I know your kind.

HUBRIS
You know what you've been taught to know. Not all of us are evil.

AVIV
And some of you devour entire villages in a fit of rage.

HUBRIS
I didn't tell you my past so you could hold it against me. I'm sure yours isn't free from it's iniquities.

AVIV
I have no god to answer to so why does it matter?

Aviv lays his head on his satchel.

AVIV (CONT'D)
goodnight.

Hubris rests his roots on a rock. We see Na'eltama'uk asleep.

DISSOLVE TO:

EXT. FIELDS OF ARABIA - NIGHT

DREAM

Na'eltama'uk stands in a field of yellow wheat. 360 visual of her in field.

She slowly walks, touching blades of wheat with her hands.

DEMONIC VOICE/SNAKE (O.S.)
(whispers)
Na'eltama'uk.

Na'eltama'uk frantically looks around.

DEMONIC VOICE/SNAKE (O.S.) (CONT'D)
(whispers)
Na'eltama'uk.

Na'eltama'uk continues to look but doesn't see anyone.

NA'ELTAMA'UK
Who are you and what do you want with me?!

DEMONIC VOICE/SNAKE (O.S.)
(louder whisper)
Na'eltama'uk.

NA'ELTAMA'UK
Show your face!

A blade of what looks like wheat from the field turns into a snake and rises to greet her, sitting on her shoulder.

DEMONIC VOICE/SNAKE
I didn't want to frighten you my child.

NA'ELTAMA'UK
You don't frighten me.

DEMONIC VOICE/SNAKE
Well, good.

NA'ELTAMA'UK
What do you want with me?

DEMONIC VOICE/SNAKE
I wanted to show you what can be yours.

Na'eltama'uk looks out into an endless field. A visualization of a beautiful village, and children playing comes to life.

She sees a WOMAN with her father's necklace on smiling at two children.

NA'ELTAMA'UK
Who is she?

DEMONIC VOICE/SNAKE
That is you my child. And your beautiful family.

TWO CHILDREN play king and queen with paper crowns on their heads. The young girl carries Na'eltama'uk's doll. Na'eltama'uk smiles.

NA'ELTAMA'UK
They're so happy.

DEMONIC VOICE/SNAKE
Don't you want to be happy?

NA'ELTAMA'UK
Of course I do.

Children run around with wooden swords looking to slay a great dragon, their voices muffled.

YOUNG PRETEND KING
Together we will conquer great lands and lead our people to power! Come! Let us claim our victory over this mountain!

They climb a tall hill of dirt. Young King sticks his sword into the dirt.

YOUNG PRETEND KING (CONT'D)
This is our mountain!

Young Queen follows his lead sticking her sword into the dirt.

YOUNG PRETEND QUEEN
Yeah, this is ours!

Na'eltama'uk laughs at children playing.

Water starts to fill empty field. She looks down at water covering her ankles.

NA'ELTAMA'UK
What is happening?!

The water rises to Na'eltama'uk's hips, covering the fields.

NA'ELTAMA'UK (CONT'D)
Take me from here!

The waters rise to Na'eltama'uk's neck. All the beautiful visions are quickly covered in a sea of blue.

DEMONIC VOICE/SNAKE
Things don't have to be this way. Na'eltama'uk.

NA'ELTAMA'UK
How do we stop it?! Make it stop!

The water rises to her chin.

NA'ELTAMA'UK (CONT'D)
Please!

The water disappears in an instant. Na'eltama'uk lays in the field of wheat.

She breathes out a sigh of relief. The snake appears beside her.

DEMONIC VOICE/SNAKE
Your creator wants you dead but I have come to give you the life you imagine and deserve. A full life.
(pause)
If you submit to me, your bloodline will not end this way. You will multiply it through sons and daughters for generations to come and you will crush the seed of Adam... I just need something from you.

Snake pulls a piece of wheat from the ground and hands it to Na'eltama'uk.

DEMONIC VOICE/SNAKE (CONT'D)
Your signature. In blood.

Na'eltama'uk takes blade of wheat. She hesitates but runs it through her left hand and opens it.

Blood comes out from a small cut in the middle of her palm.

DREAM SEQUENCE ENDS

EXT. FOREST - FIRESIDE - NIGHT

Na'eltama'uk shoots up from where she sleeps.

NA'ELTAMA'UK
No!

She looks at her hand in the light of moon. No cut is there and she sighs in relief.

DISSOLVE TO:

EXT. DYING FOREST - DAY/NIGHT

TRAVEL MONTAGE

Aviv, Na'eltama'uk and Hubris travel through dying forest.

CU on feet walking.

Na'eltama'uk's picks what's left of berries and leaves/flowers for eating. Drought has overtaken the land.

NIGHT

Aviv, Na'eltama'uk and Hubris sit by the fire as they eat a very small meal.

DAY

Na'eltama'uk finds a patch of flowers among dying forest for her oils.

CU on hands picking them.

MONTAGE ENDS

EXT. DYING FOREST - WOLF'S TERRITORY - DAY

Na'eltama'uk, Aviv and Hubris walk through a dark, ominous area of dying forest.

Na'eltmama'uk is away from the others, still picking flowers.

AVIV
Na'eltama'uk! Let's go! We should be using the flowers for food, not oils.

She turns and sees Aviv beckon her from afar.

NA'ELTAMA'UK
But what about sickness or wounds?

As she turns around she is greeted by a skinny, wild wolf. She takes a step back.

Wolf snarls and growls. She continues to step back in fear.

NA'ELTAMA'UK (CONT'D)
Easy... Easy.

Wolf snarls and slowly walks toward Na'eltama'uk.

Na'eltama'uk runs. Wolf runs after her.

Na'eltama'uk pushes back branches as she runs. The wolf is gaining on her.

Na'eltama'uk trips and turns to face the wolf. Wolf lunges for Na'eltama'uk.

An arrow from off screen pierces chest of wolf and it falls to the ground on top of Na'eltama'uk.

Aviv walks over and pulls the dead wolf off her with a smirk.

AVIV
Did you want me to save you or the oils...

Aviv offers her a hand. Na'eltama'uk takes his hand and pulls herself up.

NA'ELTAMA'UK
Very funny.

Na'eltama'uk is annoyed. She walks forward, ignoring Aviv.

AVIV
(smug)
You're welcome, by the way.

Hubris trails behind.

Aviv turns to the wolf.

AVIV (CONT'D)
We'll eat well tonight.

Aviv walks forward wolf carcass on shoulder.

CU on fur.

MATCH CUT TO:

INT. ENOCH'S HUT WINDOW - DAY

Fur from animal lays on table. Enoch finishes stretching a frame of animal skin with wooden pins and string. He tightens each wooden peg and the skin stretches.

ENOCH
Can there not be another way Father?

He tightens each wooden peg once more and skin stretches.

INT. ENOCH'S HUT WINDOW - DAY

As midday light from the window dries the animal skin, he scrapes off more with a curved knife.

ENOCH
I entreat thee, and beseech thee to grant my prayer, that a posterity may be left to me on earth, and that the whole human race may not perish.

He washes his hands seven times and dries them on a cloth by wash bowl. He sits with his scrolls.

Enoch closes his eyes for a moment. He takes a deep breath and opens his eyes. He begins to write last text.

ENOCH (V.O.)
He will give faithfulness in the habitation of upright paths.

DISSOLVE TO:

EXT. DESOLATE LANDS - DAY

MONTAGE

Aviv, Na'eltama'uk and Hubris continue to walk through desolate lands.

As they journey, land around them becomes more scarce with no sign of water.

CU on feet over changing land, dry lips, burnt skin.

ENOCH (V.O.)
And they shall see those who were born in darkness led into darkness, while the righteous shall be resplendent-

MONTAGE ENDS

EXT. DESOLATE LANDS - SUNSET

Na'eltama'uk tips a jar up to retrieve any last drops from her water. There is nothing left.

NA'ELTAMA'UK
I need to drink.

Aviv continues to lead. His lips are dried up, his eyes are tired, but he presses forward, without a thought. Hubris trails behind.

NA'ELTAMA'UK (CONT'D)
Did you hear me?
(pause)
Aviv?

Aviv continues to walk.

NA'ELTAMA'UK (CONT'D)
I know you hear me? What is this plan? To continue our journey till death? We trusted you to lead us.

Na'eltama'uk throws her empty water can at him.

NA'ELTAMA'UK (CONT'D)
Hello?!

The water can hits Aviv on the back. He stops, throws down his bag and turns to Na'eltama'uk.

AVIV
Haven't you learned the spells of Samyaza? Call on the clouds and send rain, or springs from the ground... I have done all I know to do! What more do you want from me?!

Na'eltama'uk drops her bag. Hubris approaches Aviv.

HUBRIS
Don't blame the girl.

AVIV
I will blame whomever! Do you not understand? We will die if we stop!

HUBRIS
We will die if we continue...

AVIV
Maybe this would be a good time to pray to your god and ask him why he has still forsaken you even after your turning! Where is he huh?! WHERE IS HE!?

Aviv looks up to sky.

AVIV (CONT'D)
Hello! All powerful God! How bout' a little water!

HUBRIS
Aviv, please, we...

Hubris sighs.

Aviv bends his ear to hear back from God.

AVIV
What was that God?! You're too busy?!

Hubris puts his hand on Aviv to try and bring him back down.

Aviv jerks away and chucks the empty water can at the sky.

Aviv chuckles and sits on the ground.

HUBRIS
Maybe we should rest here for the night. You're tired and not thinking clearly.

AVIV
Every day that we go without, it is becoming clear that this so called creator of the universe wants us to suffer... He could send rain now if he wanted. He could bring food if he wanted, but we, we are NOTHING to him! YOU are NOTHING to him!

Aviv gathers what is left in his bag for a fire. Na'eltama'uk rubs what's left of her lavender oil on a foot wound.

HUBRIS
I choose to believe he will provide. We must stay patient and steadfast.

AVIV
You are delusional.

Aviv tenses up, stifling frustration. He turns to Na'eltama'uk.

AVIV (CONT'D)
And will you stop it with the lavender please! I can't bare to smell it anymore!

Aviv continues to work on the fire.

NA'ELTAMA'UK
Well it's empty now.

AVIV
Good!

Na'eltama'uk rubs oil into her foot.

MATCH CUT TO:

EXT. ANCIENT MEETING SPACE MT. HERMON - NIGHT

A YOUNG WOMAN rubs oil on the feet of Semjaza against her will. She uses her long hair to wipe his feet.

ANGEL OF DARK who was spying on Noah's camp before, speaks up.

ANGEL OF DARK
I saw him. Building something of great size.

SEMJAZA
I'm not interested in taking possession of one man's property. I want resources, an army, land...

ANGEL OF DARK
He is gathering for something His God said is coming to destroy the earth.

Semjaza laughs.

SEMJAZA
Destroy the earth? That's funny.

FALLEN ONE
The Canaanites are well established. If we take up residency there...

SEMJAZA
...The women are beautiful there too.

He grabs the young woman's hand and moves it up his leg.

ENOCH (O.S.)
Stop! Let the girl go.

Voices go silent. Draped faces turn toward voice. Semjaza smiles and releases the hand of the young girl.

The girl runs off.

Light radiates off Enoch's body.

ENOCH (CONT'D)
I have come with a great warning.

Some of the fallen tremble and fall to their knees, crying and groaning. Some, including, Semjaza sit confidently.

FALLEN ONE
Who are you? Have you come to kill us?

FALLEN TWO
Please! Spare us the wrath of the father.

SEMJAZA
Get up you cowards.

ENOCH
He will come with the myriads of his holy ones, to execute judgement on all. And to destroy all the wicked, and to convict all humanity... Observe how the sea and the rivers carry out and do not alter their works from his words.
(pause)
But you... You have not stood firm nor acted according to his commandments... You have turned aside. You have spoken proud and hard words with your unclean mouth against his majesty.

SEMJAZA
God has forgotten us. We have bent our lives around His will. But what about our will?

ENOCH
Your will? You have abused your freedom and used it for evil. Women you have forced yourself upon. Men you have killed and ate of their flesh.
(MORE)

ENOCH (CONT'D)
The Lord has seen your crimes against humanity. Your crimes against all creation, teaching them your evil ways.
(pause)
Cursed be your days, and the years of your life will perish,
and the years of your destruction will increase in an eternal curse;
and there will be no mercy or peace for you!

Other Fallen Angels beg and plead and remove their head coverings.

SEMJAZA
So be it. I would rather die at his hand than live under his rule.

Semjaza smiles.

DISSOLVE:

EXT. DESOLATE LANDS - FIRESIDE - NIGHT

DREAM

Na'eltama'uk sleeps. Her eyes open in her dream world. She walks on cracked ground.

As she falls to her knees, she pulls open the cracked ground, searching for signs of water. She digs and digs with her hands.

Out from a hole in the ground appears a snake.

DEMONIC VOICE/SNAKE
Na'eltama'uk.

NA'ELTAMA'UK
Leave me.

DEMONIC/SNAKE
Leave you? But I have come to save you.

NA'ELTAMA'UK
You are a liar.

Snake hisses at Na'eltama'uk.

DEMONIC VOICE/SNAKE
Now that's not a nice thing to say.

NA'ELTAMA'UK
You showed me a future that doesn't exist.

Na'eltama'uk continues to dig with her hands.

NA'ELTAMA'UK (CONT'D)
You tricked me.

DEMONIC VOICE/SNAKE
I showed you a future... But you are not there yet.

Snake wraps itself around her shoulder/neck.

NA'ELTAMA'UK
I do not have the luxury of time. I can't afford another day without water.

DEMONIC VOICE/SNAKE
Of course, water.

Snake points his head in direction he wants her to look. Na'eltama'uk turns her head and spots what looks like a river in distance.

NA'ELTAMA'UK
Is that?

Snake slithers to ground.

DEMONIC VOICE/SNAKE
It is.

She pushes her body up and rises to her feet. She uses what energy she has left to run.

As she runs she notices she isn't moving closer to water but running in place.

Na'eltama'uk continues to run in place as tears fill her eyes.

She slows down and falls to the ground. Her head slumps over in defeat. Her eyes closed.

NA'ELTAMA'UK
Why do you torment me?

DEMONIC VOICE/SNAKE
Na'eltama'uk, my child. I will be sure that your desires are satisfied.

NA'ELTAMA'UK
When will they be satisfied?! I don't believe you!

DEMONIC VOICE/SNAKE
I can see that your broken spirit needs some convincing.

Snake circles around her. As it slides across the ground it creates a small trench. It fills up with water.

Na'eltama'uk cups her hands in water and drinks until she chokes from drinking to fast.

DEMONIC VOICE/SNAKE (CONT'D)
Now do you believe me?

Snake continues to create lines/trenches around Na'eltama'uk.

Na'eltama'uk continues to drink with desperation.

DEMONIC VOICE/SNAKE (CONT'D)
Here...

Na'eltama'uk looks up. Demonic snake has shape shifted into a DEMONIC MAN holding a leather water skin.

Na'eltama'uk rises to her feet and takes the leather water skin.

She drinks from it and water leaks from sides of her mouth.

NA'ELTAMA'UK
Thank you.

DEMONIC VOICE/MAN
Of course my child. And in return I thought that you could give me something.

NA'ELTAMA'UK
You have my signature in blood, what more do you need?

DEMONIC VOICE/MAN
Your word.

NA'ELTAMA'UK
My word?

DEMONIC VOICE/MAN
I need to know that you are committed to me. To the bloodline.

NA'ELTAMA'UK
Fine. You have my word.

DEMONIC VOICE/MAN
Good.

God's eye view of the trench in the shape of an upside-down pentagram.

Na'eltama'uk stands in the middle.

DREAM ENDS

DISSOLVE TO:

EXT. DRY LANDS - DAY

Aviv cups sand/dirt in his hand and lets it sift through to tell what direction the wind is blowing.

He points east. Hubris and Na'eltama'uk trail behind, desperate for water.

NA'ELTAMA'UK
(whispering to herself)
Where is the water you promised me?

Na'eltama'uk licks her lips to relieve the dryness/cracking.

NA'ELTAMA'UK (CONT'D)
(whispering to herself)
I gave you my word. Will you not deliver yours?

Aviv looks back and sees them trailing behind.

AVIV
You have to keep up!

Na'eltama'uk sees mirage of Demonic Man from dream.

NA'ELTAMA'UK
(to sky)
Where is the water you PROMISED ME!?

Na'eltama'uk falls down and grabs sand/dirt in both hands. Aviv goes to her side.

AVIV
Get up.

NA'ELTAMA'UK
I can't.

Na'eltama'uk continues to dig with desperation.

AVIV
We will die if we stop.

NA'ELTAMA'UK
There has to be water here! He said it!

Na'eltama'uk arms grow tired of digging. Na'eltama'uk hangs her head over the dirt/sand.

NA'ELTAMA'UK (CONT'D)
(to the ground)
You promised me!!

Hubris grabs Na'eltama'uk. He places Na'eltama'uk on his back. They continue to walk forward.

Na'eltama'uk lays on her back looking at sky.

NA'ELTAMA'UK (CONT'D)
(exasperated)
You promised.

--

Aviv and Hubris walk. Na'eltama'uk lays on Hubris's back with her eyes open. She sees a white dove flying over.

Na'eltama'uk closes her eyes and screen goes black as eyes close.

ENOCH (V.O.)
My warnings had fallen on deaf ears.

DISSOLVE:

INT. ENOCH'S HUT - DAY

Enoch places the last of his writings in leather bags for safe keeping.

ENOCH (V.O.)
I prayed it would be different. I prayed for their turning, but not one of them did.

KNOCK KNOCK.

METHUSELAH (O.S.)
Father...

METHUSELAH (Enoch's son in old age), enters.

The two embrace.

ENOCH
Safeguard these writings... bring them to your Noah.

Enoch hands him a bag of scrolls.

METHUSELAH
Yes Father. We should pack your things. The time is drawing near.

Methuselah grabs some of Enoch's belongings and begins to pack them. Enoch places his hand on his sons.

ENOCH
My body cannot make the journey.

METHUSELAH
But you must.

ENOCH
It's okay my son.

METHUSELAH
I cannot leave you here, alone.

ENOCH
The Lord will be with me. Really, it's okay...

The two embrace again.

ENOCH (CONT'D)
We will see each other again soon.

Enoch holds his son and closes his eyes.

MATCH CUT TO:

EXT. SOMEWHERE NEAR THE EUPHRATES RIVER - DAY

Na'eltama'uk opens her eyes. She looks to the right and sees what looks like greenery/water.

Tears fill her eyes.

NA'ELTAMA'UK
Put me down... Put me down.

Na'eltama'uk falls off the back of Hubris, to the ground.

HUBRIS
Na'eltama'uk...

Aviv and Hubris watch Na'eltama'uk run ahead not seeing what she sees.

AVIV
Where is she going?

HUBRIS
I have no idea.

Na'eltama'uk continues to run toward water with hope filled eyes and wide smile.

Na'eltama'uk cups her hands in the water to drink and laughs tears of joy.

Aviv and Hubris continue to walk in the far distance. Aviv squints his eyes in disbelief.

AVIV
I can't believe it...

Hubris smiles and looks up.

HUBRIS
Thank you.

Aviv and Hubris run toward the water. They fall in and their bodies emerge. Hubris branches comes back to life again.

Aviv bathes in water and drinks it.

HUBRIS (CONT'D)
Coincidence or answered prayer?

AVIV
Whether it's from the gods or the earth, I really don't care.

Na'eltama'uk dunks herself under water. She stays there for a moment taking in water around her. She shoots up from the water.

Hubris's branches regain more leaves. The three continue to enjoy water for a little while.

Longer beat.

All Tribe Member dialogue in unknown language.

TRIBE MEMBER 1 (O.S.)
Out!

The three look toward the voice. A cannibal HUMAN/ANIMAL TRIBE MEMBER with mask, dressed in blue/white war paint carrying a spear stares them down.

His TRIBE behind him stares.

TRIBE MEMBER 1 (CONT'D)
Out! You have trespassed on our waters!

Aviv pulls his hands out of the water and extends them in peace.

AVIV
We are just passing through. We will be on our way.

TRIBE MEMBER 1
Out of the WATER!

AVIV
Okay, okay...

Aviv gets out of water and walks toward the tribe.

Na'eltama'uk and Hubris follow behind. The all hold their hands up to signal peace.

AVIV (CONT'D)
Peace.

Tribe members point their spears and look at Aviv with evil intent.

They confer.

TRIBE MEMBER 1
What are they?!

Tribe members yell out.

TRIBE MEMBER 2
His skin is pale and dead! He is a dead man walking. A dead man walking!

Aviv places hands together and bows to give respect to Tribe Member 1 and gain trust.

AVIV
Peace.

TRIBE MEMBER 2
White witch. And hair, burnt by the sun!

They pull on Na'eltama'uk's hair.

NA'ELTAMA'UK
Peace! No war, peace.

Na'eltama'uk places hands together and bows to give respect to Tribe Member 1.

TRIBE MEMBER 2
She has placed a spell on us!

TRIBE MEMBER 1
(repeating English)
NO. Peace. NO!
(unknown language)
White witch...Ghost of man. Tree beast... You walk OUR land! These are OUR waters you drink from!

AVIV
We don't understand.

Tribe encircles them. They extend their spears toward their necks.

Tribe moves in irefully with a synchronized movement and loud chanting.

ALL TRIBE
(chanting)
Eat of their bones, drink of their blood! Eat of their bones, drink of their blood!

TRIBE MEMBER 1
(chanting)
Bring Nomed!

Tribe summons their giant leader.

ALL TRIBE
(chanting)
Nomed! Nomed!

NOMED (half animal, man-giant) roars loudly. His tribe uses sinew strands to bind Aviv to the back of Hubris. Nomed pours acid on Hubris's roots.

It burns and boils. Hubris roars in pain. Na'eltama'uk tries to run to Hubris but is struck down by Tribe Member 1.

Nomed picks up Na'eltama'uk.

NA'ELTAMA'UK
Let me go!

Na'eltama'uk tries to push herself from his grip. Nomed laughs.

They are led back to camp of cannibal tribe.

DISSOLVE TO:

EXT. CANNIBAL VILLAGE - FIRESIDE - NIGHT

Aviv and Hubris sit by a fire, hands and legs tied.

Tribal drums are played as the ceremony begins. Tribe members chant and dance around.

All Tribe Member dialogue in unknown language.

ALL TRIBE
(chanting)
Eat of their bones, drink of their blood! Eat of their bones, drink of their blood!

Tribe Member 1 paints face of Na'eltama'uk white.

Drums, music and chanting stops.

NOMED
We call on the power of the dead! May the blood of these sacrifices grant us many days of life!

Drums hit.

TRIBE MEMBER 1
May it give our people the strength of the gods!!

Drums hit three times. Music continues to play.

DANCING TRIBE MEMBER, dressed in colored hay and palm fronds from head to toe, dances with enchanting movement.

Aviv peers over to Hubris, trying to signal him.

AVIV
(whispered)
Hubris... Give me a hand.

Aviv tries to loosen the ties.

Hubris reaches around to try and help but doesn't have the strength.

HUBRIS
I am too weak.

He tries again.

AVIV
(softly)
We cannot back down now! What about Na'eltama'uk? Have you forgotten your promise?

Hubris sees Na'eltama'uk standing before the tribe in all white, including white face paint. She is escorted to what looks like an alter.

Music and drums continue to play. Hubris tries to cut Aviv's ties again. Part of the ties are cut.

Drums stop.

NOMED
Ancestors! Come to us!

Drums hit.

ALL TRIBE
Come to us!

NOMED
We present this sacrifice to you!

ALL TRIBE
Come to us!

Drums hit.

TRIBE MEMBER 1
Grant us passage through Sheol!

ALL TRIBE
Come to us!

Drums hit. Music and drums continue to play.

ALL TRIBE (CONT'D)
Come to us!

Dancing Tribe Member takes smoke and dances around Na'eltama'uk to prepare her body.

A large curved sword wrapped in silk is brought to Tribe Member 1 and unwrapped. He grabs curved sword.

Drums hit three times.

Music/drums continue to play.

Aviv struggles to untie his arms behind his back as ceremony continues.

He cuts a long piece of her braided hair. Na'eltama'uk closes her eyes and breathes deeply.

JUMP CUT:

EXT. NA'ELTAMA'UK'S HUT - DAY

DREAM

Sister braids Na'eltama'uk's hair while Na'eltama'uk braids her dolls hair.

SISTER
Your mother had red hair just like this... I'm not as good at braiding as she was.

Sister finishes.

SISTER (CONT'D)
There... And look, you and your doll are twins.

JUMP CUT:

EXT. CANNIBAL VILLAGE, FIRESIDE - NIGHT

Na-eltama'uk opens her eyes. She sees her hair taken fireside.

TRIBE MEMBER 1
(chanting)
Shaleawa' shaleawa' shaleawa' te meh toga!

Tribe Member 1 puts a piece of hair in a bowl over fire. It burns up.

Drums hit three times.

Tribe Member 1 dances around Na-eltama'uk with sword.

TRIBE MEMBER 1 (CONT'D)
(chanting)
Shaleawa' shaleawa' shaleawa' te meh toga!

Aviv finally rips apart his tied hands then quickly rips apart his tied feet.

He disarms nearby tribesman and sends spear through his chest.

Music stops.

Aviv stumbles into the clearing and finds himself face to face with Nomed.

Nomed immediately strikes toward Aviv with his sword. Aviv blocks.

Aviv and Nomed trade blows with their weapons at a furious speed before Aviv knocks him to ground and cuts Na'eltama'uk free.

Nomed recovers and strikes Aviv. They trade blows and Aviv is knocked to ground dropping his sword.

Na'eltama'uk throws Aviv his sword and Aviv pierces Nomed.

Two other Tribesman run toward Aviv and Na'eltama'uk to attack them. Na'eltama'uk picks up a spear.

They strike sending both Tribesmen to the ground killing them.

Na'eltama'uk cuts ties off Hubris. Hubris stands with what strength he has left.

360 inside circle of Tribesmen surrounding Aviv, Hubris and Na'eltama'uk.

Tribesmen engage in combat with spears.

ALL TRIBE
(chanting)
Shaleawa' shaleawa' shaleawa' te meh toga!

Hubris throws men as they charge him. Aviv battles with spear and sword in hand knocking enemy tribe members to the ground and piercing them.

Injured Nomed gets up from the ground and goes head to head with Aviv.

Na'eltama'uk and Hubris continue to fight off Tribesmen in background.

Nomed slashes, Aviv parries. Nomed blocks countermove and thrusts his weapon forward.

Aviv blocks and parries. Nomed ripostes. He kicks Aviv to the ground.

Nomed stands over Aviv in defeat. He lifts his sword to finish Aviv.

Na'eltama'uk pierces Nomed from behind. He falls to ground and Aviv slowly stands to his feet.

NOMED
Cursed be the ground you walk upon!

Nomed dies.

Aviv nods to Na'eltama'uk.

AVIV
Returning the favor, I see.

NA'ELTAMA'UK
You're welcome.

AVIV
We need to move.
(pause)
Hubris?

Hubris tries to follow but doesn't have the strength.

AVIV (CONT'D)
We are almost there.

HUBRIS
I can't.

Na'eltama'uk grabs flowers from a nearby bush and tries to crush them to make oils.

NA'ELTAMA'UK
You're gonna' be okay, I promise.

HUBRIS
It's okay Na'eltama'uk.

Na'eltama'uk puts a small amount of oil on his roots. One breaks. Hubris winces in pain.

HUBRIS (CONT'D)
Save your oils.
(pause)
For your journey.

Hubris looks to sky and sees two white doves flying west. Na'eltama'uk and Aviv see them too.

HUBRIS (CONT'D)
I am at peace here. You can leave me.

NA'ELTAMA'UK
We cannot leave you!

HUBRIS
I never thanked the birds for their songs... Never thanked the rain for it's drink. Or the sun for it's growth. I hoarded the fruit of my branches. Held onto my leaves in the coldest of winters.
(pause)
I never realized there was health in surrender.

NA'ELTAMA'UK
Hubris, you must get up, please!

Na'eltama'uk tries to pull Hubris to his feet. Hubris looks at her apologetically.

HUBRIS
God has been so merciful with me yet I never postured myself in his light, only my own.

NA'ELTAMA'UK
You will be better tomorrow okay? Aviv we can't leave him here, help me carry him.

Na'eltama'uk tries to pull him with her own strength. Na'eltama'uk falls to the ground trying to carry his weight.

NA'ELTAMA'UK (CONT'D)
Don't just stand there! Help me!

AVIV
Please, let him die in peace.

Aviv comes to Hubris's side.

AVIV (CONT'D)
Wherever death meets you, I pray it rewards you for your bravery.

HUBRIS
Don't let my body be wasted here. Use my branches for your fires; a vessel to carry you on your way. Promise me.

AVIV
You have my word.

Na'eltama'uk lays her head on Hubris.

HUBRIS
It's okay my child.

Hubris takes one last breath in and out.

HUBRIS (CONT'D)
It's okay.

Hubris dies.

NA'ELTAMA'UK
(to herself)
I led him here, this is all my fault.

--

AVIV
Na'eltama'uk, you cannot carry the weight of his death on your shoulders. There is no way to have known that these waters would lead us here.

Na'eltama'uk takes a seed from the leaves on Hubris's branches.

She kneels to the ground and digs a hole with her hands. She places the seed in a hole and covers it with dirt.

Aviv gathers water to saturate the ground. He pours it on area where seed is planted.

AVIV (CONT'D)
His death will not be the end of him.

DISSOLVE TO:

EXT. EUPHRATES RIVER - DAY

Aviv and Na'eltama'uk travel on a makeshift raft made of reeds/papyrus/wood down Euphrates River with their bags, supplies, food and wood.

To the right of the Euphrates we see two of many types of young animals walking in the same direction.

NA'ELTAMA'UK
Where do you think they're going?

AVIV
I don't know, but they do.

To the left of the Euphrates we see two of many different types of young animals walking in the same direction.

NA'ELTAMA'UK
They're everywhere.

CUT TO:

EXT. EUPHRATES RIVER SHORE - DAY

SUNSET

Aviv pulls the raft ashore. Na'eltama'uk watches animals pass by.

NA'ELTAMA'UK
I think they are going where we're going.

AVIV
It's possible.

NA'ELTAMA'UK
Maybe they sense something coming.

Na'eltama'uk looks up at the dark clouds forming. Aviv puts up makeshift tent.

AVIV
Will you grab me a few rocks?

Na'eltama'uk travels down to waters edge and gathers a few rocks.

As she picks up second rock a cobra raises its head/neck off ground and moves toward Na'eltama'uk.

Na'eltama'uk places hands out. She remembers the song of her ancestors that calmed the snakes.

NA'ELTAMA'UK
(singing, Hebrew)
Hush my sweet serpent, hear my sweet call. Lead forth your children from cave to my shawl.

DISSOLVE TO:

EXT. FIELD - NIGHT

FLASHBACK

A snake comes into view. It sits in front of young Na'eltama'uk (toddler). It is quickly hypnotized by music/song.

NA'ELTAMA'UK
(singing, Hebrew)
No pain will come to your shining scaled brood. I sing you to sleep...

JUMP CUT:

EXT. EUPHRATES RIVER SHORE - DAY

SUNSET

NA'ELTAMA'UK
(singing, Hebrew)
In your sanctuary wood.

Snake backs down for a moment. Na'eltama'uk lowers her hands and walks backward.

She trips over a bush and Snake reengages charging forward.

Aviv intervenes and Snake strikes his foot, drawing blood. He grabs the snake by the neck and rips it in half.

AVIV
Are you alright?

NA'ELTAMA'UK
Me? Are you alright?

AVIV
I've been bitten by many snakes. The venom of a bellied beast is no match for Nephilim blood... Come. Let's eat.

Na'eltama'uk picks up two rocks to bring back to the tent.

CUT TO:

EXT. SHORELINE FIRESIDE - NIGHT

Aviv and Na'eltama'uk eat cooked snake.

Aviv takes a big bite and chuckles.

AVIV
Taste like lavender.

NA'ELTAMA'UK
I'm sorry.

Long beat.

AVIV
Whenever I came home, she would wrap me in warmth. Her hair, always smelled like lavender. She was such a beautiful woman. Hated war just like you. Wanted to be a mother more than anything. I hate that the thing she wanted the most took her from me... And in God's cruelty he took my son too.

NA'ELTAMA'UK
You would have made a great father. And I'm sorry for your loss.

Aviv takes a deep breath and finishes his food. Na'eltama'uk sees a snake eat a white dove.

AVIV
What is it? Na'eltama'uk?

It disappears as if it was never there.

NA'ELTAMA'UK
My visions. They're becoming more and more frequent. And I worry that I've made a mistake.

AVIV
Visions are just visions. They aren't reality.

NA'ELTAMA'UK
The things I have seen and the things I have done are very real to me.

AVIV
Right here, now. That is what's real.

NA'ELTAMA'UK
What if the sorcerer's warnings are true and I have followed the wrong path? Maybe that's why everything has been going wrong and...

AVIV
...This is the path our fathers would have wanted us to take. We must do everything in our power to protect the bloodline.

Aviv puts his hand on Na'eltama'uk's shoulder.

AVIV (CONT'D)
Trust yourself.

DISSOLVE TO:

EXT. NEAR THE ARK - NIGHT

DREAM

Storm clouds accumulate over a dark sky (TIME LAPSE). Great waters rush over local towns/villages. Waves crash.

DISSOLVE TO:

INT. ENOCH'S HUT - NIGHT

Enoch shoots up from his bed breathing heavy and sweating. He folds his hands in prayer.

ENOCH
Father. Be with me.
(pause)
Quiet my mind.

Enoch looks up.

ENOCH (CONT'D)
Give my heart peace. For I know what is coming.

Enoch is beamed up in a great light.

CUT TO:

EXT. EUPHRATES RIVER - DAY

The light of the sun beams down on Aviv and Na'eltama'uk as they travel down river.

In the distance, Na'eltama'uk sees a large ark 90 percent built.

NA'ELTAMA'UK
Aviv, look.

Aviv looks. Animals surround the ark. Larger animals lift cargo and wood to help build remaining parts of the ark.

EXT. METHUSELA'S TOMB - DAY

Noah's family is gathered around a tomb.

NOAH
My grandfather brought great wisdom. He was a man of virtue and honor. He served our family and God with conviction and compassion. I am thankful that he didn't have to endure what is to come in these next days. He is with the father.
(pause)
He is at peace. Let us pray...

Aviv and Na'eltama'uk into the tomb, hearing voices out of their view. They follow.

AVIV
Pretend to by my daughter.

NA'ELTAMA'UK
What do you mean?

NOAH (O.S.)
As we bid farewell to our beloved Methusela, God grant us the strength to bear the weight of this grief.

Aviv and Na'eltama'uk continue, the voices growing, their curiosity peaking.

AVIV
We are strangers on their land. If I am your father, they will show compassion toward me.

Na'eltama'uk nods.

NOAH (O.S.)
May his legacy and faith live on in our hearts and in the stories our children tell... Amen.

Noah and his family bow.

FAMILY
Amen.

Noah sees Aviv and Na'eltama'uk as he opens his eyes. He turns to his family.

NOAH
The time is drawing near. We must press forward.

His family continues to build. HAM (Noah's son) makes eyes with Na'eltama'uk. Noah approaches Aviv and Na'eltama'uk.

NOAH (CONT'D)
Interrupting a burial, you sure know how to make a first impression.

AVIV
Apologies.

Aviv bows head.

NA'ELTAMA'UK
Our condolences.

Na'eltama'uk bows head. Noah summons his daughter in-laws.

NOAH
Take care of the girl. Fetch her water to bathe and give her something fitting to wear.

SIBYL AND OTHER WIFE take Na'eltama'uk's hands and walk her to a tent.

Ham makes eyes with Na'eltama'uk again as he carries wood in background. Ham eaves drops on his father's conversation.

AVIV
We were sent here to help. We have traveled many days and nights without food and water.

Noah laughs, looks back at the almost done ark.

NOAH
I don't know that we need your help.

AVIV
I offer my daughter Na'eltama'uk as a gift.

HAM
Father. Let them stay.

NOAH
Son, please. Back to work.

Ham goes back to preparing wood. Noah ponders his son for a moment.

NOAH (CONT'D)
My son Ham is without a wife. I will go to the father in prayer. If it is His will, tonight, Ham will ask for your daughter's hand and we will celebrate the Lord bringing Him a companion.

DISSOLVE TO:

INT. TENT - NIGHT

The girls adorn Na'eltama'uk with beautiful colored silks.

SIBYL
You would make a good wife.

NA'ELTAMA'UK
Oh I'm not ready to be married.

SIBYL
No one is ever truly ready.

Sibyl and Other Wife prepare Na'eltama'uk's skin with oils.

NA'ELTAMA'UK
This seems like a lot for just cleaning up.

SIBYL
Ham is a good man.

OTHER WIFE
Yes he is.

NA'ELTAMA'UK
Who?

SIBYL
Your father has given his blessing and you will marry Ham, son of Noah.

Na'eltama'uk confused, defensive. Sibyl and Other Wife place a silk veil over her head.

NA'ELTAMA'UK
Marry Ham? But I have never met him.

SIBYL
Trust that God has brought you here for a reason and respect your father's wishes.

Sibyl positions Na'eltama'uk's veil just right.

SIBYL (CONT'D)
Ham will love you.

NOAH'S WIFE comes in, carrying Na'eltama'uk's bag.

NOAH'S WIFE
Here is your bag of things...

The doll falls out. Noah's wife picks up and looks at it.

NA'ELTAMA'UK
It is the cloth of my mother and the necklace of my father.
(MORE)

NA'ELTAMA'UK (CONT'D)
My mother died giving birth to me.
My father, well...

Na'eltama'uk catches herself. Noah's wife pulls off the necklace from the doll and ties it around Na'eltama'uk's neck.

NOAH'S WIFE
Your father will be proud to see you in this.

NA'ELTAMA'UK
May I have a moment. Please.

Na'eltama'uk eyes well up with tears as she holds her necklace.

QUICK CUT:

EXT. TENT - NIGHT

Na'eltama'uk runs off. Veil falls and travels in the wind to the feet of Aviv standing with Ham.

Aviv goes after her but Ham stops him.

HAM
I will see to her.

Na'eltama'uk runs through wooden area, pushing through branches. She runs into a Dark Angel Spy with black veil. He raises his sword to her.

Ham raises his sword, lunging forward at the spy.

Dark Angel side steps countering with a swift slash that barely misses.

Tension builds. Dark Angel progresses, drawing a false sense of security.

Ham launches a fierce counterattack but is quickly growing tired.

Dark Angel countermoves sending Ham to the ground. He stands over Ham and raises his sword.

Na'eltama'uk knocks Dark Angel in the head with nearby rock. He falls to the ground.

Na'eltama'uk reaches out her hand to help Ham up. They have a bit of a spark.

DISSOLVE TO:

Fire burns under a night sky. Na'eltama'uk stands in front of Ham. Aviv is at the fireside looking down.

Noah stands before Ham and Na'eltama'uk.

NOAH
And with these rings, let them be an outward symbol of your eternal commitment to each other in love and service.

Ham places the ring on Na'eltama'uk's finger. She looks up at him.

HAM
(whispering)
You are beautiful.

Na'eltama'uk smiles but looks away quickly. She places a ring on his finger.

NOAH
Let us pray.

Everyone prays.

NOAH (CONT'D)
Father in Heaven, we celebrate the union of Na'eltama'uk and Ham. We ask that you go before them and guide their steps. Let nothing come between this bond and their bond with you. Amen...

Everyone claps in celebration. Noah's sons play a song of celebration on their instruments.

Ham smiles at Na'eltama'uk.

HAM
(whispering)
I promise to protect you all the days of my life.

Na'eltama'uk looks up and smiles at him, then looks back down. He pulls her hand and leads her in a ancient dance.

At first she is hesitant to dance but warms up to it. Aviv is seen retreating to woods in the background.

At end the of dance Ham holds her close and the two look into each others eyes with more passion.

EXT. SOMEWHERE NEAR NOAH'S CAMP - NIGHT

Noah follows Aviv.

NOAH
You should be celebrating yet you look conflicted.

AVIV
Seems normal for a father to feel the weight of his decisions and hope that what he has chosen is best.

NOAH
I understand.

Noah grabs Aviv's shoulder.

NOAH (CONT'D)
You are a good father, don't be so hard on yourself.

AVIV
I don't know that I am good.

NOAH
We are good because of God's goodness.

AVIV
God wants nothing to do with me.

NOAH
Would you be here if that were true?

Aviv looks up into the night sky pondering Noah's words.

MATCH CUT TO:

EXT. HUT - NIGHT

A blanket of stars stretch over a night sky.

INT. HUT - NIGHT

Na'eltama'uk lays beside Ham covered with blanket. Ham is asleep covered.

DARK SHADOW enters hut. It breathes heavily.

NA'ELTAMA'UK
(whispering)
What do you want with me?

Dark Shadow quickly shifts from one side of room to other. Na'eltama'uk's eyes follow in fear.

NA'ELTAMA'UK (CONT'D)
How long will you torment me? Have I not followed your plan?

Dark Shadow jumps on top of Na'eltama'uk and covers her mouth. She tries to breath/speak, but can't.

DARK SHADOW
Your body is mine.

She tries to get up but can't. She grabs for Ham's hand.

Ham finally awakens and sits up. Na'eltama'uk sits up quickly, Dark Shadow disappears.

HAM
What is it? Are you okay?!

NA'ELTAMA'UK
My dreams are crippling.

Ham holds her.

HAM
It's okay. You're safe here.

Ham draws on her back as he holds her tightly. Na'eltama'uk takes a deep breath in and out.

NA'ELTAMA'UK
I just want them to go away. But I fear they will stay with me forever.

HAM
I have dreams that burden me too. My father said it's both a blessing and curse to have a gift like that. I pray that yours becomes more of a gift and less heavy on you.

NA'ELTAMA'UK
I pray that too.

DISSOLVE TO:

INT/EXT. NOAH'S ARK - DAY

Men finalize last parts of ark on outside and inside. Animals move in and are positioned in different areas.

AN ENEMY MESSENGER travels by horse to deliver a message to Noah and his family. He is far in distance but Noah notices.

Na'eltama'uk gathers water for the men. She hands a cup to Aviv and he drinks it.

NA'ELTAMA'UK
Lavender water. Your favorite.

AVIV
I see you're still mad at me. Everything I have done was for your good.

NA'ELTAMA'UK
My good?

AVIV
Na'eltama'uk.

NA'ELTAMA'UK
No. You are not my father and had no business giving my hand in marriage.

AVIV
(whispered)
Shhhh. Do you want to get us killed?

NA'ELTAMA'UK
(loud whisper)
You vowed to protect me and this is the best plan you could come up with?

AVIV
You're alive aren't you?

NA'ELTAMA'UK
You were protecting YOU. Not me.

AVIV

This was always part of the plan Na'eltama'uk... To carry out the bloodline. A way to win without physical war, the way you wanted it.

NA'ELTAMA'UK

That's all you care about, the bloodline.

AVIV

So you don't care?

(Pause)

Fine. Then we have traveled for nothing and our fathers have fought and died for nothing and Hubris died for nothing...

NA'ELTAMA'UK

Don't do that.

AVIV

Do what?

NA'ELTAMA'UK

Put all the burden on me. What weight is yours to carry?

AVIV

The sorcerer told you it would be this way.

Na'eltama'uk walks away.

AVIV (CONT'D)

Na'eltama'uk.

Aviv goes back to carrying wood to Noah who is working on final construction of ark.

Aviv looks up and sees Enemy Messenger coming closer.

AVIV (CONT'D)

Noah.

NOAH

I see him.

AVIV

Who is it?

NOAH
Another obstacle trying to keep me from the task at hand.

Noah looks up to the Heavens.

NOAH (CONT'D)
My bones are weary and tired Lord. I don't know how much more I can take.

AVIV
Just say the word and I will take care of it.

NOAH
I don't want war Aviv.

Messenger rides up to Noah.

NOAH (CONT'D)
How can I help you?

ENEMY MESSENGER
I have a message from Akkad... And this will be his final words to you: cease this foolishness or meet the wrath of our great army.

NOAH
You tell Akkad I cannot and will not go against my creator, God.

Thunder roars.

NOAH (CONT'D)
He has spoken and given me direct orders. I will be obedient to finish the work he has called me to do.

ENEMY MESSENGER
Then you have sealed the fate of your family.

NOAH
My family will be protected.

Enemy laughs.

ENEMY MESSENGER
Is that so? We will enjoy taking your women for ourselves, then killing you.

Enemy Messenger rides off. Noah continues to work. Aviv continues to work.

Dark clouds hover over.

DISSOLVE TO:

EXT. SOMEWHERE NEAR THE EUPHRATES RIVER - NIGHT

Young animals walk in twos to the ark.

Long beat.

TIME LAPSE OF NIGHT TO DAY and animals walking.

MATCH CUT TO:

EXT. ARK - DAY

Animals travel onto the ark. Noah reaches out his hands and touches them on the head as they enter the ark two by two. One of his other sons and Aviv help lead them onto ark.

NOAH
This is the last of them. They will go to the east wing. Be sure the food trough is stocked and water is ready to go.

OTHER SON
Yes Father.

Noah watches a circle of dark clouds stir above. A drop of rain falls on his face and lingers.

NOAH
(to himself)
It's coming.

INT. ARK - HOLDING AREAS - DAY

Other Son and Aviv help navigate animals into holding/sleeping areas.

Aviv helps fill their food troughs with hay and fills a few water jars that are low.

AVIV
Unbelievable.

OTHER SON
When my father started building I thought he was crazy. But I have seen God's hand in all of it. It's amazing, the animals know the voice of their creator.

Aviv continues filling the water and food in animal troths, thinking about the miraculous things he just saw.

OTHER SON (CONT'D)
If only we could listen the way they do.

EXT. ARK - DECK - DAY

Noah continues to hammer the last of the nails in.

Rain becomes more fierce. Sounds of thunder.

Aviv steps out to the deck. He sees something coming in the far distance.

Aviv sees Enemy Tribe coming towards the ark with many men/giants. He turns to Noah.

AVIV
You must get in the ark, now.

Noah nods. He and his family gather what's left of their belongings.

The Enemy Tribe gets closer, trudging through heavy rains.

AVIV (CONT'D)
Go, now!

Aviv grabs his sword and walks away from Ark toward army of men in the rain.

Na'eltama'uk runs after him.

NA'ELTAMA'UK
Where are you going?!

Aviv turns back to address Na'eltama'uk.

AVIV
I have to do this!

Na'eltama'uk grabs his arm to stay.

NA'ELTAMA'UK
You don't have to fight anymore.

AVIV
Last time, promise.

Aviv smiles and walks away. Na'eltama'uk tries to go after him but is stopped by Ham.

Aviv runs into enemy territory as he fights off first of the men and giants, killing them.

The sound of steel rings out as swords clash. Sounds of thunder. Lightning strikes in the distance.

Aviv fights with everything he has but the sheer number of his opponents overwhelms him, his defenses crumbling.

He looks back and yells.

AVIV (CONT'D)
Shut the door! Now! GO!!

Noah's son hesitates, torn between obeying and aiding Aviv. The family tries to turn the pulley system to shut the door but can't.

With a final, desperate surge of strength, Aviv manages to fight off many, buying precious time for Noah and his family.

Aviv looks back and realizes the door isn't closing.

A mighty wind and waters bursting from the ground slam the door shut. Aviv is filled with hope. He yells out a battle roar and slays a few more of the enemy as waters rush around him.

He is hit by an arrow on his right shoulder. He pulls it out and continues to fight. He is hit by a second arrow to the heart.

His knees hit the ground and he lays there.

Na'eltama'uk screams out. Ham holds her close.

Semjaza stands over Aviv's broken body.

AVIV (CONT'D)
It is done.

Water shoots out from the ground around them. Rain falls heavy from the sky. The water surges forward crashing over Semjaza, then Aviv and those remaining.

INT. ARK - DAY

The ark rocks aggressively and heavy winds are heard. The Family is seated and strapped in holding hands.

Long beat.

Na'eltama'uk holds tight to her necklace.

In the corner of the ark are many scrolls.

CU on scrolls.

DISSOLVE TO:

TEXT READS: on that day all the springs of the great deep burst forth, and the floodgates of the heavens were opened. And rain fell on the earth forty days and forty nights. Genesis 7:11-12

TIME LAPSE

Show floodwaters gradually receding over many days/nights. The land becomes less barren and begins to vegetate again.

EXT. EUPHRATES RIVER DAYS/NIGHTS - TIME LAPSE CONTINUES

A sapling sprouts up by a familiar river's edge, its roots taking hold of damp soil. It grows into a young tree and then older, its branches reaching upwards.

TIME LAPSE ENDS

FADE IN:

EXT. SHRINE OF THE BOOK ISRAEL MUSEUM - DAY

SUPER: PRESENT DAY

Fountains spring up from around the museum.

INT. SHRINE OF THE BOOK, ISRAEL MUSEUM - DAY

TOUR GUIDE gives a tour. Group looks at old scrolls.

TOUR GUIDE
And they are considered one of the most important archaeological discoveries of the 20th century.

They continue viewing ancient writings.

TOUR GUIDE (CONT'D)
Here, we are dedicated to preserving and conserving these ancient writings. Everything from temperature to lighting, storage and restoration are handled by an expert team with care.
(Pause)
This ancient jewish religious text is the Book of Enoch. Attributed to Enoch, a biblical figure mentioned in Genesis. Scrolls were discovered by a young boy looking for his goat.

A few in the group chuckle over the goat comment.

An ELDERLY WOMAN (80s), frail but with a keen gaze, lingers behind the group, her eyes drawn to the Enoch artifacts and a picture of young Muhammad the Wolf.

Discreetly, she reaches up and grasps the necklace resting against her chest - the same leather strap and stone pendant we saw earlier on Na'eltama'uk.

TOUR GUIDE (CONT'D)
This book contains visions, prophecies and teachings including descriptions of heaven, the earth, angelic beings known as the watchers or fallen angels, their children the Nephilim and the concept of the Messiah.

TOURIST
Are the nephilim a people that still exist today?

TOUR GUIDE
Great question. Some would argue they were all wiped out entirely during the great flood, as that was the divine intention... to cleanse the earth from the wickedness and corruption brought on by the fallen.
(MORE)

TOUR GUIDE (CONT'D)
Other scholars propose that the Nephilim survived the flood through Noah's family. It is believed that their bloodline, influence and control still remain today... Any more questions?

Elderly Woman stands there a moment, lost in thought, fingers trace the worn leather.

TOUR GUIDE (CONT'D)
Good, moving on you'll see we have the book of Giants.

The speech of the tour guide becomes muffled and distant as Elderly Woman slowly exits.

TOUR GUIDE (CONT'D)
It provides additional details about these mysterious hybrids and their role in the events leading up to the great flood.

As elderly woman walks, she glances back one last time at the museum, a flicker of memory crosses her weathered features before she turns the corner and disappears from view.

FADE TO BLACK.

THE END

Acknowledgements

I would like to extend my heartfelt gratitude to the Fifth Estate Publishing team—Breandan, Joseph, and Robert—for their inspiration and encouragement as I ventured into historical fantasy writing for the first time. A special thanks to Joseph Lumpkin for his expertise in theology, guiding me to sacred texts and scholarly commentary that ensured the theological elements of my original story were aligned.

To my amazing husband and wonderful children, your endless inspiration and support fill my life with joy and creativity. Because of you, my stories come to life, and I am grateful for the fun and adventure we share together. To my mom and dad, thank you for your constant love and support, and for always giving selflessly so that I could pursue my passions and dreams, even when resources were limited.

I also want to express my appreciation to the teachers who saw beyond my learning disability and encouraged me to tell stories; your belief in me made all the difference.

It is my hope that as you read this script, the characters and their journeys will inspire you to reflect on your own spiritual path, wrestle with weighty questions of faith, and ultimately find connection. May it stir something meaningful within you.

www.ingramcontent.com/pod-product-compliance
Lightning Source LLC
Chambersburg PA
CBHW030414310726
48979CB00002B/417
* 9 7 8 1 9 5 8 4 5 0 1 4 7 *